RAISING
HELL

BRYONY PEARCE

RAISING
HELL

uclanpublishing

Raising Hell is a uclanpublishing book

First published in Great Britain in 2021 by
uclanpublishing
University of Central Lancashire
Preston, PR1 2HE, UK

978-1-912979-54-7

1 3 5 7 9 10 8 6 4 2

Set in 10/16pt Kingfisher by Becky Chilcott.

A CIP catalogue record for this book is available from the British Library.

Printed and bound in Great Britain by Clays Ltd, Elcograf S.p.A.

To the class of 2020
At least there weren't zombies . . .

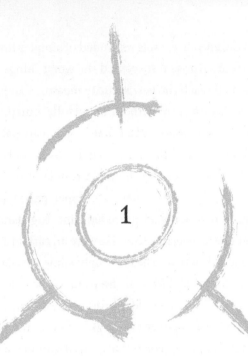

1

IT WAS THE goths you had to watch out for. Not that they were any more likely to snap than anyone else, at least in my experience. In fact, they seemed to have a healthy outlet for all that angst, but *they* tended to hide among the goths; in plain sight.

I stopped checking out the noticeboard (someone was selling what looked like a decent second-hand laptop) and turned my attention towards the little group walking through the metal detector. What should a group of goths be called? A flock? A herd? I remembered the old joke about a murder of crows. A murder of goths? No, not right. A slaughter perhaps. A slaughter of goths.

I shifted Matilda on my hip. I hated having to carry a huge machete, especially in my old school. Every morning when I approached the entrance, I was reminded of simpler times – when a low grade or a surprise test seemed the worst things that could happen. Then I'd reach the new security measures and tell myself only a fool dealt with goths without being fully armed.

First through was a boy. Black hair, obviously; pale make-up and bruised-looking eyes that remained dull as he looked me over. Even though I'd only been in the job a couple of months, I had already become part of the scenery. He sloped past, following the preppy-looking trio that had preceded him, bag dangling from one shoulder like an overripe fruit. He wore an earbud and nodded along to a tune only he could hear. A slight smile raised the corners of my lips. I knew him, although he wouldn't remember me. I'd been in the same class as his older brother a few years ago.

Behind him, a pair of overweight girls, new to the look; make-up too carefully applied, hair recently dyed and inexpertly – like they'd used boot polish on it. Black jeans not yet frayed, layered tops, grateful to slink into the colour. They giggled; hadn't yet got the style of careless rebellion.

I nodded at the closer of the two as she looked me over, nervous eyes going first to Matilda, then to the mirror, flare, Bible, lighter and canister of holy water that were tucked into my flak vest. As I shifted my stance, the little bell on the other side of my belt jingled. I sighed at the Christmassy sound but fortunately, in this case, size genuinely didn't matter.

Still, perhaps I should invest in something that rang lower down the tonal scale.

Wannabe-goth-girl lowered her gaze and clutched her friend's arm. They whispered, both stared at me and then at the floor – then they were gone.

What had scared them the most, I wondered? Was it the equipment that reminded them of my job, or was it that I looked like Nancy Drew on a bad hair day: slight frame, big brown eyes. I appeared more curious than uncompromising and was no one's idea of an ass-kicker.

Perhaps they were worried that I wouldn't be able to protect them when the time came. Not *if… when*. I had no illusions about my role here – it was to put my body between kids not that much younger than I was, and the inevitable.

Worse, I had a feeling I'd be earning the 'danger money' part of my wage sooner than I'd hoped. There had been a rash of in-school attacks with worrying similarities recently, and they seemed to be building up to something. I'd always been good at spotting patterns, and the stories that had made the news were raising my hackles. Someone was using disaffected kids to cast offensive spells, if only I could work out what they were using them *for*.

The last through was another girl. Long black hair, as per the uniform, but this time it had the sheen of a natural colour or at least a professional dye job – it fell around her thin shoulders as though oiled. Pale make-up, but her eyes, beneath the painted-on rings, were sharp and clear. They said, *'I'm better than you and I know it'*. I straightened.

'You.' I pointed.

She froze, looked at me. 'Me?'

'Bag check.'

Arched eyebrows came together. 'I've done nothing wrong.' Her accent was upper class with cut-glass syllables. Offended.

'It's random. Your number came up,' I lied, and gestured to the table beside me. 'You can unload here.'

3

'I'd rather not, thank you.' The girl turned and began to walk away. She looked as if she'd snap in a high wind.

I stepped into her path, two long strides, and unclipped the machete with one hand. 'I'm afraid this isn't optional.'

Two groups were gathering – the boy and two girls who had been with my target had stopped to wait. Behind her, a line of students shuffled with increasing impatience towards the detector.

'Get out of the way!' A stocky lad, rugby ball under one arm.

'Just doing my job,' I snapped, without even looking at him.

The girl's eyes met mine; they said 'asshole' and I felt a flicker of mutual understanding. Then she spoke in a lowered tone. 'I've got *personal* items in here. I'm sure you understand.' She smiled, so charming. 'I don't want guys like *that* to see, you know.'

'It's your time of the month?' I spoke in a normal volume and watched to see her reaction.

She bit back the comment she wanted to make. I watched her swallow the words like bitter sweets. Such self-control – very *un*-teenaged. 'Yes,' she said eventually. 'Yes, exactly.' She moved to go past again.

'Sorry.' I stepped once more into her path and pointed at the table. 'Bag check.' I enunciated very clearly.

'You're kidding me?'

I shook my head.

'I have rights.' The girl gripped her bag like it contained her grandmother's tiara.

'Sorry, but you don't. Not here. Not now.' I let her look at Matilda again, still in her holster, but no longer clipped in place, and I took the girl's elbow to guide her towards the table. Her bones were sharp, almost protruding. 'What does it matter if *I* get a look at your *personal items*?' I kept my voice calm but sensed it wouldn't do any good. This girl wasn't worried about a few tampons and a packet of Nurofen. Not this one.

My instincts were good, and they were standing up and screaming.

'Norah, what's the haps?' The boy called out, his tone tired, like he could barely be bothered.

'Go on without me.' She didn't even look back.

I held her eyes – establish dominance, that was the first thing. Make her *believe* she had to do as I said, even though I was only three or four years older than she was. The hairs on my arms were standing up, and goosebumps stippled my chest. It wasn't cold, but I was chilled. The noises of the hall fell away. It was only me and the girl.

'Name?' I asked as I took her bag from her. She tried to hold on to it for a moment longer then finally allowed me to take it, her long fingers twitching as if she wanted to snatch it back.

'Norah Ortega.' She tossed her hair. She was going to try and brazen it out. *'I don't know what they are.' 'How did they get in there?'* or even, *'They're for a history project.'* Honestly, I'd heard it all.

I licked the dying felt tip I'd been issued and made a note on my list: *06.01.2025, 0837, Norah Ortega, bag check.* She was the first of the day, tenth on the paper. The ink almost ran out when it reached her name, rendering it ghost-like on the form. I shook the pen, licked it again and finished.

'Ortega?' There was something about that name. I'd heard it before.

She shrugged. I looked down at the rucksack I had won.

Purple, not black, but marked all over with indigo sharpie. I peered closer. Signs and sigils.

I sighed. 'Do you know what these are?' *I* recognised them of course: Protection, Security, Distraction. Anyone else would have had their attention diverted if they'd considered opening the bag. The girl watched to see what I'd do. I reached for the zip and she tensed. Her wards hadn't worked, not on me. It was the main reason a nineteen-year-old had been given the security job in the first place.

I looked at her again and her sharp dark eyes blazed. She wanted to know who I was, *what* I was, but she daren't ask.

'Do you know what these are?' I repeated.

She shrugged. 'Copied them from a book. They seemed cool. You know, the whole *look*. Obviously, they don't *do* anything.' She was pissed off.

'Yeah.'

It *was* possible. I'd recently been in a firefight where it *had* been a genuine accident. Some teens from my building copied a bunch of hieroglyphs from the internet, thinking it was hilarious. It's all fun and games till somebody gets eaten.

I pulled open the bag expecting to see the usual: a witch's pouch, a sack of herbs. Perhaps a voodoo doll or a pentagram made from twisted yew twigs, that kind of thing. There was nothing. I skipped over the books: text-books, library books. I rifled through the pencil case: pens and pencils, a sharpener, rubber, set square, protractor, not even a compass for me to comment on. I frowned. A small make-up bag in a side pocket. I checked it. Dark grey eye shadow, pale powder, purple lipstick. I put it back. There was a lunchbox and a bottle at the bottom. I popped it open.

Two sandwiches, a bag of crisps, an apple, a chocolate chip cookie. I sniffed the bottle.

'Water?'

'It's healthy.' The girl reached for her things. Smug. 'Can I go to class now?'

'Wait.' I caught her wrist and stared at the open bag. My gut was tight now, a knot of balled pain. I was missing something. I put my hand right down and felt for lumps, hidden pockets. Perhaps it was something tiny: an artefact, a ring, a locket.

Still nothing.

What hadn't I seen?

I looked at the girl again. She had all the signs. All my experience told me I was right. Maybe it was *on* her?

'Empty your pockets.' I folded my arms.

The girl sighed, but this time she wore an air of satisfaction. I'd missed it – whatever *it* was. I watched with a sinking heart as she emptied detritus on to my table. A phone, a handful of loose change, a tissue, a small wallet which, when opened, proved to contain only a credit card, a bus pass and a real photograph of a younger girl whose dark brown hair was in lopsided bunches. Finally, she produced an orange plastic hair clip that didn't match her outfit and a wrapped sweet stuck to a business card.

'What's this?' I picked it up and turned it over. There was just a single word: *Emporium*.

'Nothing important.' The girl had hesitated so I knew she was lying.

I slipped the card into my flak vest.

The girl scowled and started to repack her bag.

'Yo, Ivy. Can I get this line moving now?' It was the guard at the metal detector. Bristling moustache and floppy dark hair. Thought of himself as the John Wick of the school corridors – fingers always twitching over his gun stock.

I itched all over. What was I missing?

'Yeah, I suppose.' The girl had beaten me. I could hardly strip search her. Wait – jewellery could be worn.

'Let me see your fingers.' I caught her hands. They were cold in mine and her fingers were bare. I turned them over – her nails were filthy.

I pulled her nearer and looked at her throat. No necklace. No rings.

We both knew this was a game and I had lost. My throat felt scratchy as failure burned all the way down. Maybe it wouldn't be so bad. It was possible she was only hiding a love spell, or a beauty charm. Perhaps *this* failure wouldn't mean some innocent died. I almost choked on my own delusion.

She smiled. She'd been hiding in plain sight and she'd got away with it . . .

My brain finally made connections. Hiding in plain sight. As she tossed her pack over her shoulder, I grabbed the dangling strap and pulled her back.

'Let me just see something.'

'Ivy, come *on*, already. Let her go.'

'One more minute, Charlie.'

The girl's smile faltered. 'You've seen everything. This is harassment.'

'Just a last quick check, then you can go.'

She held her breath as I opened the bag again and lifted out the library books. Two gothic horrors – surprise, surprise. One book on genus and species and a thin, but heavy tome titled *The Rise of the Samurai in Feudal Japan*.

Odd. With trembling fingers, I pulled off the dust jacket. Underneath, the title was something very different.

'Bloody hellfire.' I reached for my machete.

I was too late.

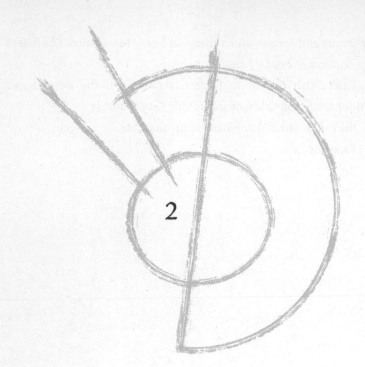

2

TERRIFIED SCREAMING MADE me drop the book. It was with only slight satisfaction that I saw the gothed-out boy shrieking wildly and retreating up the hallway.

I glared at Norah. 'I'll deal with you *after*.'

The tome lay on the tiled floor, pages flipping as if in a heavy breeze.

I had no time to secure it. As Norah reached down, I kicked the book out of her reach, and it spun towards Charlie. 'Don't let her get hold of it,' I yelled.

'John Wick' stared at me, then at the thing in the hall. He was pale as milk, trembling and reaching for his gun.

'The *book*, Charlie!' I screamed. I had no time to baby the man through this; any moment now, kids were going to start dying.

I pulled my machete and leapt over the table. Goth-bitch was trying for the book again, so I elbowed her to the floor as I sprinted past. She cried out as she landed hard on hands and knees and I smiled grimly.

'*Char—lie!*' I howled. He blinked as if waking from a dream and I saw him bend down. Good, I could give my full attention to the slaughter.

Goth boy was already at my side, grabbing my arm, gabbling incomprehensibly. Automatically I checked him over, no blood, no gore – no problem. I shoved him out of my way, and he flew towards Norah. Let her deal with him.

Now my view down the corridor was unobstructed, I paled.

I still ran forward though. The two overweight goths were pinned against a wall, too terrified to make a sound. Silent tears were streaming down their faces, leaving pink tracks in their make-up.

Whistling through my teeth, I slowed. I wanted to run back the way I had come, but it wasn't as though I had a choice. The thing stalking the girls was the size of a bear, and black in a way that sucked at the light. It seemed darker in the hallway where it stood. Its eyes were holes, with single glowing pinpoints deep in the pit of them. It started snarling, and there was the colour; yellow fangs the size of pencils, ridged pink gums, scarlet tongue. Saliva pooled on the floor.

Behind it, the shadows were gathering into the form of a second beast. Thankfully it wasn't yet solid, but it would materialise on to this plane soon enough. I had to move fast.

I glanced back. 'How did you raise *two* hounds?' I yelled. Norah was staring past me, her mouth open, her eyes wide and shocked.

I mean the sheer power that was needed to raise just one hound . . . I'd never even seen a fully corporeal one in real life before.

Students were no longer trying to get through the metal detector, instead they were jammed in the doorway battling to get out. Charlie was finally waking up. He held the book in one hand and his gun in the other.

'Stay back,' I cried, but he had John Wick on the brain and was swaggering towards me, his jaw set.

'Shit,' I muttered. I took a deep breath, forced a sprint and, just as the first hound bunched its hindquarters to bound at the girls, I leapt, with my machete held high.

I didn't cry out as I attacked, hoping the hound would keep its attention on the girls, but as my feet left the ground it sensed me coming and turned. Its eyes bored into mine.

For a heartbeat I was falling into a pit of darkness – all around me were howls and wails, as I waded through blood and excrement and . . .

Sneaky. Note to self: do not make eye contact with a hell hound.

I returned to my body in time to slam on to the hound's back with my legs on either side of it, as if I was sitting on a horse. Hair like barbed wire bit through my jeans as I drove the machete between its shoulder blades. The beast's low growl turned into a whine as the blade stuck and it snapped at my hands, vicious in its pain. It couldn't reach me, and it spun, crazed with rage. I risked a glance at the second hound. It was more solid, its eyes now glowed from the shadows, but it was not yet ready to attack.

The girls hadn't moved.

'Run!' I yelled, and finally they grabbed one another and escaped sideways.

It was like holding on to the world's most brutal rodeo bull. I gripped Matilda's handle with one hand and the hound's mane with the other, ignoring the way its pelt sliced my fingers, as the hound bucked and twisted. Then I was slammed into the wall, the air rushing out of me, as it tried to scrape me off. Which wasn't a huge problem, I mean, I wanted to get off but I had to do it safely.

Suddenly a building collapsed on my leg. A gunshot echoed from concrete to tell me what had happened.

'You moron, Charlie! You shot me . . .' My bloodied hands slid from the machete handle and I thudded to the ground, back first, struggling to get my breath. Then the hound was on me.

More gunshots. I rolled into a ball, hands behind my neck, trying to protect my softer parts. I was all too aware that my leg was pouring blood and driving the hound into a frenzy. Its roar was more lion-esque than dog-like and I felt the first bite as its razor teeth sank into my arm and it shook me, trying to get to my guts. I curled up more tightly as I was dragged around the floor, like a bloody balloon leaving trails of gore. Its saliva sped into my veins, burning as if it had injected acid.

More gunshots.

'You're just making it angry!' I choked, but I knew Charlie couldn't hear me.

There was screaming all around me now; kids watching me get mauled, running footsteps.

'Give me the book!' It was Norah, trying to get to Charlie. I didn't dare look. Did he have the tome secured? If she got hold of it . . .

The girl was sobbing, sounding genuinely upset. Ha! 'I have to—'

The bell on my belt jingled as the dog hurled me into a wall and something in my arm tore.

I star-fished as I hit an art display, and the dog moved like lightning. Its teeth sliced into my flak vest, just above my kidneys. Then it whined and pulled back. Smoke billowed from its mouth and its gums bubbled. Stuck to its upper fangs was my two-inch-thick King James Bible.

'Serves you right,' I gasped. Wasting no time, I rolled between its feet and scrambled towards Charlie on one hand and one elbow, ignoring the blood that dripped from my, now useless, arm and the red handprints I was leaving on the floor.

Norah was wrestling with the security guard, trying to pull the book from his hand.

The hound shook its head to dislodge the Bible and when I felt something hit my skull, I knew it had succeeded. Slipping in my own blood, I rolled and put a boot in the air, knowing the hound would be coming after me.

I managed to kick it in the muzzle and knock it sideways.

Another gunshot and the beast started to retreat. Charlie was finally having an effect.

There was a yell of female triumph behind me. I didn't dare look, but I knew what had happened.

I grabbed the bell from my belt and shook it hard. The jangly sound shouldn't have been audible above the hound's snarls, the screaming of the students and now Norah's chanting (the cow)! Yet it was. The hound shook its head as though a bee had flown into its ear.

My left hand wasn't working, I put the crown of the bell between my teeth and shook my head, keeping the sound coming. Then

I yanked the flare from my vest before the beast could recover. I popped it with my thumb, and it sparked into life.

The chanting behind me was horrible. What was Norah trying to achieve? One thing at a time. I forced the flare into my lifeless hand, wrapping my own nerveless fingers around it and hoping they would hold. Then I took the bell out of my mouth. The Bible was lying open between my legs, at Leviticus. There was a smoking hole clear through the centre and I smelt burning paper.

'Bell,' I cried and shook it again, hard. 'Book.' I nudged the Bible. 'Candle.' I couldn't raise the flare, but I held it and that's what mattered. Then I started the incantation, raising my voice to try and drown out Norah's garbled intonations.

'In the name of God, the All-powerful, Father, Son and Holy Ghost, of the Blessed Peter, Prince of the Apostles, and of all the saints, in virtue of the power which has been given us of binding and loosing in Heaven and on Earth, I exclude you from the bosom of Earth, declare you anathematised and judge you condemned to eternal fire. I deliver you to Satan.'

With that, I rang the bell one last time and dropped the flare on the floor where it sputtered out.

There was an odd quiet. The students who remained in the building had fallen silent and were watching with wide eyes and pale faces. Charlie was standing, legs spread, his gun held in both hands, trained on the beast. The only sounds were the dripping of my blood and the drone of Norah's voice as she chanted in the background.

The hound snarled, low in its throat; its muscles bunched and strained, but it couldn't move. I used the wall to get to my feet. I noticed, worriedly, that I couldn't feel my right leg.

I lurched drunkenly towards the hound, one arm hanging loosely at my side. Its eyes, those holes into hell, followed me – red pits glowing with banked fury. I reached out and wrapped my hand around Matilda. I pulled and the hound growled, making all the hairs on my neck stand up.

'I need her back,' I said, almost conversationally. The machete was jammed into bone and there was no moving it.

'Charlie, help!' I turned to see the security guard, shaking his head, a frantic no. 'Charlie, you shot me. Get over here!'

A more definite no, this time.

I groaned and put my leg on the wall, leaning back as I yanked at the blade. Female whimpers behind me. As if they were suddenly all worried about the doggy.

It was like pulling the sword from the stone, but Matilda finally came free with a crunch of bone and an arc of crimson blood. The hound quivered but couldn't move. I'd made sure of that.

I tucked Matilda back in her holster and started to back away again, towards the Bible.

'It's nothing personal,' I said, 'But you're going back to hell.' I kicked the Bible shut with one foot.

The hound popped out of existence with an anguished howl that tolled down the hall, reverberating like the aftermath of an explosion.

One down. I leant on the wall between the noticeboard and the Year Eight field trip display, and stared at the second hound. It was starting to growl, but I could still see the doors to the new science block through its flank. I had a moment. I was bone-tired – exhaustion was a weight on every limb, but I unsheathed Matilda and raised her in a shaking hand. I was going to be right there, ready to start hacking as soon as it was solid enough to cut.

But the chanting was getting louder.

Suddenly Norah pushed in front of me. She was holding the book out in front of her like a shield. I wobbled. There *was* one way to stop the second hound from attacking. One way to end it all right now.

I lined the blade up with the base of her neck.

NORAH BENT OVER the tome and her hair parted to reveal her pale nape, almost as if she was offering herself as sacrifice.

My arm trembled. I was meant to save kids, not kill them. And I was hardly an angel myself. But if I didn't stop her, how many more would die?

I couldn't do it. I shrieked my frustration. Norah didn't even turn. Her voice vibrated in my head, getting louder and harsher. Latin syllables clashed against one another, one moment almost familiar, the next like no language on Earth.

The hound growled louder.

Fricatives and sibilants burst from her tongue like overripe berries. I smelt my own blood mixed with the scent of hell: sulphur and shit, or was that the bouquet of high school? Somewhere behind me students were running again; classroom doors slammed, but it wouldn't matter. If the hound got past me, it would chase them down.

Was this what had happened in Manchester? The news said investigations were ongoing, but a hellhound could have caused the damage.

I didn't want to hurt anyone, but ... wait, there *was* another way? I reversed the machete and hammered the handle into the back of Norah's head. She dropped like a stone and the *Necronomicon* hit the floor, falling open on the page she had been reading.

Only then, as the hound howled, did I realise my mistake. With a triumphant snarl the monster burst into life.

'Oh *no!*' I dropped to my knees, abandoned Matilda and grabbed the book, dragging it towards me. Norah hadn't been calling the hound, she had been trying to hold it – to send it *back*. Guess she had a conscience after all. Or, more likely, once I'd found the book, she worked out that she'd be spending a long time in prison for this particular high-school massacre.

The hound was going to reach Norah before it got to me. I had a choice, protect the girl or keep reading. It was no choice at all. I rubbed blood out of my eyes and focused on the pages. The writing was spidery, the text close set and difficult to read. My vision swam, and fatigue dragged at my eyelids. It had been a while since I'd seen a copy of this book. But once upon a time I'd studied it, as if it could stave off the end of the world.

My body was telling me I needed to shut down, to heal. I punched myself in my wounded thigh and the pain that burst through me like a firework shot me back to life.

I started to sound out the Latin phrases – not smoothly, but loudly, making sure to sound out every letter.

'Fluxus converterent . . .'

The hound leapt straight over Norah as if it didn't see her.

'Claudeturque porta . . .'

Its scalding breath blew on my face, the stench burned my nose. I was crying now, fat tears dropping soaking into yellowing paper. I had to keep reading, until the very end.

Why hadn't the hound gone for the closest victim? I blinked as I focused on Norah and her backpack. 'Of *course*!' How far did the power of her protection and distraction sigils extend? I threw myself between the hound's legs, landing face down on the girl as if she was a mattress, fitting my legs to hers. The pack dug into my chest. The hound's teeth snapped at my hair, tangling in my ponytail with a sharp tug; then it whined. I kept the *Necronomicon* clutched tightly in front of me, my eyes on the blurring words. I kept reading, whispering now, even as the skin on my back wanted to crawl around to my front as I anticipated the talons that were about to slice into me.

'*Fluxus converterent. Claudeturque porta.*'

Confused whimpers above me. Saliva dripped in my peripheral vision. The hound had feet like plates and its claws ticked on the tiles as it searched for me. With a whine, it licked my blood off the floor. I suppressed a whimper of my own and kept reading, repeating the words. Third time the charm. Literally.

'*Fluxus converterent. Claudeturque porta!*'

The beast bayed and, unlike the first, which had just winked out of existence, banished cleanly, this one was dragged into an invisible vortex, its howls piercing. A hurricane seemed to fill the hallway, but there wasn't even a breeze to dry the sweat on my forehead. As I watched in quiet horror, the hound came apart; skin dragged from bone, muscles exposed, guts unreeling. A swirling tornado of gore.

I gaped until the very last – when the final piece was pulled into the whirlpool. My ears popped and then, silence.

Sound rolled back in – sobbing, a long tear as the weight of the damaged display pulled it from the wall, the thud of feet on concrete, the sound of sirens outside. Beneath me, Norah twitched, and I rolled off her with a groan, coming to rest on my back. One hand remained on the *Necronomicon*, the other touched Norah's own outstretched fingers.

The fluorescent light above me was flickering; no pattern to it. On off, on off, then a pause; on, off. I stared, unable to turn my head. My leg was numb, and my arm throbbed. I could still feel the hound's saliva burning in my veins. I lay completely still, bruises aching. My thighs felt sandpapered.

After a while, the face of a policeman appeared above me. I watched him take in my damaged vest, equipment and Matilda lying a few feet away.

At least he didn't say anything stupid, instead he switched on his radio. 'I need some paramedics in the hallway and two stretchers.' He went to his knees beside me – his eyes were the same blue as his uniform, and he needed a shave. 'Everything is going to be all right,' he lied.

✳ ✳ ✳

Gripping my crutch, I hobbled through the metal detector. Matilda knocked against my thigh and the alarm went off, but Charlie didn't even try to stop me. He glanced at my bandaged leg and my arm in its sling and his eyes skidded away, shamefaced. He'd had a haircut.

What he couldn't see was the thudding burn that accompanied every beat of my heart, and he couldn't hear the faint growling in my ears, that the doctor claimed was tinnitus.

The school was empty – it would be a few more days before it opened again. There were, however, several cars in the car park. Some belonged to the cleaning crew who, now the forensic team had vanished, would finally be getting around to bleaching my blood off the floor. The rusting muscle car was Charlie's, of course, and the rest belonged to the governors who were, presumably here to thank me for stopping their students from becoming dog food. In the far corner, another vehicle caught my attention. A twelve-foot long all-black limo that looked as if it was about to take off: sleek, slick and shining. A bald-headed beast of a man stood in the gloom beside it, as if to attention. His suit looked nailed on. I frowned. Who arrived at a high school governors' meeting in a limo driven by a wrestler? For myself, I'd been dropped off in a taxi. It was going to be a few weeks before I could drive my trusty old Yaris again.

To be honest, it seemed like overkill to have a special meeting. I'd rather have enjoyed the rest of the fortnight at home like the students and saved the taxi fare, but here I was.

I'd been asked to go to the new science block for the engagement; the headmaster's office was too small for more than three people and the hall was too echoing big.

I stared at the double doors that led to the new build. There was a plaque on the right-hand side, shiny like the handles: *Sponsored by Ortega Enterprises*. My heart lurched. I *knew* I'd seen that name before. Had someone wanted me to see this before the face-to-face? I suppressed the thought and pushed the doors, grateful that this part of the school held no memories for me.

There was a staircase in front of me. I sighed as I looked at the stairs and then at my crutch. My leg still hurt but I was healing. Steps shouldn't be a problem; they just weren't any fun. I climbed, huffing and puffing.

As there was no sign of anyone else, I showed the pain I was in – my lips turned down and my eyes tightened. Then I was at the top of the stairs and I leant on the wall to get my breath back, schooling my expression back into one of careful professionalism. These guys paid my salary after all and what with the bonus I was expecting today, it was worth keeping them friendly.

I limped down the corridor, my crutch ticking against the tiles. It was a chilly morning and the sky outside the windows I passed was solid with cloud – grey and looming. The lights had been switched on and their eerie brightness washed out my skin, making the hand curled inside the sling, appear dead and cold.

The department still had a new paint smell, but the scent of sulphur tickled the back of my nose: residue.

As I got closer to the biggest classroom, I could hear voices, low and rumbling. So, they had been there for a while before me. I hadn't meant to keep anyone waiting.

The door was cold against my hand and it resisted me for a moment, before swinging open. Inside, the governors were separately grouped, it seemed, by gender. The women: older, rigid hair, leaning towards plump. The men: balding, bespectacled and besuited. The headmaster sat on his own near the back. I'd only met him a couple of times. It had been Mrs Venn when I'd gone here, but she'd retired not long after I'd left, unable to cope with a world where the teaching profession could be literally cursed for giving a failing grade, or distributing what a teenaged spellcaster considered too much homework.

Teachers had suffered the highest number of casualties in the last four years.

In the centre of the room, as out of place as a lion in a field of zebra, there was a man who seemed only a few years older than I was. He sat on one of the kid's stools as if it were a throne, with one ankle crossed over the opposite knee. He had shining shoes, black socks and grey wool trousers. His shirt was white and crisp. He had no jacket. His long hands dangled over his folded leg. He was relaxed. My eyes travelled upwards and he tensed – his broad shoulders twitched, and a fist clenched. What? Didn't he like my outfit? It wasn't exactly easy to get dressed, with a gunshot wound and a broken arm, but I had pulled on my very best tracksuit bottoms for this meeting. And the logo on my T-shirt was hardly offensive. Perhaps my bandages bothered him?

I took in a face with a sharp line of dark stubble, perhaps two days-worth deliberate growth. His cheekbones had edges like Matilda. His jaw was wide and strong, his eyes sharp and so dark they were almost pupil-less. His hair was black, *goth* black. I swallowed, abruptly wishing I'd brought Matilda from the car. But this was a governors' meeting for cripes sake. I was here for the grateful thanks of the population.

I cleared my throat and the men turned.

'Ah, *Miss* Mann.' The oldest smirked as if my name was a joke he had just told, one I'd never heard before. He took a long stride forward, moved to shake my hand, saw my injuries and his

24

eyes widened. 'We weren't told . . . I didn't realise.' He glanced accusingly at the silent head and grabbed a chair. 'Sit down.'

I started towards him, then hesitated. No one else was sitting, only the dark-haired stranger and the head. I shook my head. 'I'm fine, really.'

'Good, um, great. That's . . .' He coughed and looked around. 'Perhaps then . . .'

The loudest of the women strode to his side. She wore a long lilac jacket over a pleated skirt and strong perfume – fruity and too young for her. Her skin was shiny and claggy with face powder. She folded her arms.

'Miss Mann, I'm Irene Worth. We need to speak about the . . . incident . . . that took place the other day.'

Although Mrs Worth obviously intended to lead the meeting, my eyes slid from her like she was oiled and landed once more on the younger man who remained silent, one finger tapping the heel of his shoe. A shoe that had cost more than my whole wardrobe. I touched my elasticated waistband and blinked. Who was he? My empty hand curled at my belt. Where I usually kept Matilda.

'Yes, the . . . incident.' The older man caught my attention again. 'We were told . . . hellhounds. I mean, the danger to the school.' He stroked his moustache. 'It's the worst episode we've had in three years.'

I nodded. In my short time in the job I'd dealt quietly with a portal to who-knows-where, that had opened in the cafeteria, a cursed library book that had taken out three students before I tracked it down and, what had appeared to be, civil war ghosts emerging from a grave under the hockey pitch (it was the round helmets that had given them away, my old history teacher would be proud and shocked that I'd spotted that). Not to mention the daily grind of love charms, hexes and truth spells that make life in high school so much more interesting than it had been when I was there.

'I got it under control. A few of the kids were scared sh— I mean *frightened*. Really frightened, but not hurt.'

The young man rose to his feet, like an oak growing under time-lapse photography. 'Not hurt?' He frowned, his expression darkening so much that I turned to protect my injured leg and arm. My fingers twitched again: no Matilda. Automatically I checked the room for possible weapons – heavy stools, test tubes that could be broken to provide blades. And I had my crutch. I pulled my sleeve down over my palm and loosened my knees ever so slightly. His eyes narrowed.

The governors shuffled, aware of some change in the atmosphere. A snap in the air.

'Nothing serious, surely,' Irene trilled.

'If you call a concussion "nothing serious".' The man took a step closer to me. I shifted my balance to my good leg.

'The students escaped.' I frowned. 'There was no—'

'Norah Ortega *is* a student.' He sneered. 'Isn't she worthy of your protection?'

I gaped. 'Are you serious?' I looked at the governors, who avoided my gaze and shifted to take up position behind the man – a semi-circle of censure. The head still said nothing, looking out of the window as if something in the car park interested him greatly. I'd get no help there. 'You're not . . . are you?' I frowned. 'She raised the hounds in the first—'

'Where's your proof?' The man growled. 'According to my

witness, she was trying to *stop* the hound when you hit her. With a machete.'

I swayed. I hadn't been prepared for this. I'd been expecting a handshake and a bonus. But this?

'She had the book, she called the houn—'

'She had *a* book.' He took a step nearer and I edged backwards. 'You injured a child without knowing all the information, without checking.'

'Only the book that opened the portal would have the counter—'

'Surely there are more copies of that particular book – I understand that it's quite famous.' The stranger loomed over me. I could smell his aftershave – spice and musk. He had muscles under that shirt. I lifted my crutch off the ground.

I sucked in my cheek. 'In theory,' I admitted. 'Perhaps. But if she intended no harm, why bring the *Necronomicon* to school?'

He ignored this. 'My sister was trying to help you. Bravely attempting to banish a hell hound, when you hit her hard enough to hospitalise her.' He leant forward, my personal space had gone.

'Your . . . sister?' My mind started to turn. 'Mr . . . Ortega?' I thought of the plaque and my heart sank. It didn't matter what the girl had done. I was going to be the one who paid.

'Yes.' The man faced the governors but spoke to me. 'Did you *see* her cast a spell to call the hounds?' His confidence was supreme.

I glared at his back. 'A spell like that . . . she'd have had to come in to school the night before, set it up at midnight, ready to trigger when the students started arriving. I wouldn't have seen—'

'She was at home the night before,' Ortega snapped. 'With me.'

'Are you sure?' My leg was aching now, I needed to move. I remained still. 'Teenagers—'

'She's my *sister*.' He addressed the governors. 'You said *if* she was able to convince you. Has she?'

Mrs Worth looked at her folded hands; plump knuckles, rheumatism on the way. 'N—no,' she stammered. 'But look at her, Mr Ortega, her commitment to protecting the school – surely—'

'I want her gone.'

I straightened. 'What?'

He whirled and his eyes burned into mine. He pointed. 'I. Want. Her. Gone,' he repeated. 'My sister could have been killed thanks to that trigger happy—'

'I don't even carry a gun!' I exclaimed. 'But I did get shot.' A flush was rising, reddening my chest, climbing up my throat and bringing waves of heat. 'And *your sister* tried to murder the student body!'

'She tried to *save them*.' He curled a lip and tossed words over his shoulder at the governors, like grenades. 'Fire her!'

I swayed. 'If you fire me, I won't be able to get a job in another school. I'll be considered too dangerous. I'll never get a job in security again. You *can't*.'

'What if she resigns.' Mrs Worth said, her voice brittle. 'Her employment prospects . . .'

'You want her working around more children?' Mr Ortega shook his head. 'No.' He lowered his voice so that only I could hear. 'You hurt my family, Miss Mann. I love my sister very much and so now I intend to *destroy* you.'

I lunged and brought up my crutch. Ortega barely moved, but his hand clamped around the shaft, holding it still like it had hit rock.

'See,' he said to Mrs Worth. 'Miss Mann is a liability. It was only a matter of time before she hurt a student.'

'I . . .' Mrs Worth wrung her hands, and then I remembered.

'You're Olivia's mother aren't you, Mrs Worth?' I tried to ignore Ortega. 'There was an incident in my first week on the job . . .'

Mrs Worth gasped and flushed, looking quickly at the other governors. 'It was nothing.'

'Certainly nothing that needed reporting to the Commission.' I limped closer to Mrs Worth as the other governors looked at her with narrowed eyes. I lowered my voice. 'If I hadn't saved the other girl's voice though, it would have needed to go much further.'

'What do you want?' Mrs Worth hissed.

'I help children,' I breathed. 'I helped your daughter and the girl she hexed. It's what I do. Don't fire me.'

Ortega clapped his hands together. 'Enough!' He looked over to the governors one more time. 'Let me make myself clear,' he said quietly. 'Future donations from my family are dependent on Miss Mann being removed from the premises. Permanently. Fired with no references.'

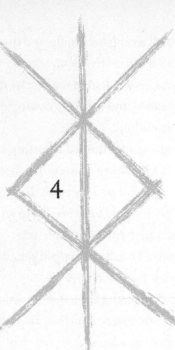

4

'I WAS RIGHT, WASN'T I? You got a juicy bonus, didn't you? How much? Are we going on holiday?'

Grandma was waiting on the doormat. As I opened the door, she curled herself around my ankles with no concern at all for my injuries. I shook off the sling – I didn't really need it at this point – then bent and stroked her absently, my mind racing.

'I'd like to take a cruise,' she carried on, barely stopping for breath. 'I never managed one while I was alive. Your grandfather, you know. He hated sailing. Selfish ass-hat.' She leapt on to the sideboard and batted at my crutch. 'The Caribbean,' she purred. 'And I'm out of food.' She looked meaningfully at her empty bowl.

'I fed you before I left,' I said and leant tiredly against the door. 'You'll get fat.' Where was I going to get another job? More importantly, where was I going to find a job that would allow me to *atone*?

'That's a very rude thing to say.' The cat butted my hand and forced me to scratch her under the chin by turning her head. 'You know I'm sensitive about my weight.' She batted me with claws out and I winced. 'Anyway, it's hungry work.'

'What is?' I frowned at her.

'Do you have any idea how many rats there are in this building?'

'None.' I rolled my eyes. 'There's never been a single rat.'

'Yes, but there could be.' She twisted to force my hand along her spine. 'You have salmon in the fridge,' she purred.

'That's *mine*.'

'Thankless child.' She pulled away and glared at me. 'You know how I feel about cat food.'

'But you eat it.'

'It's that or *starve*,' she yowled. 'The way you treat your own grandmother, it's a crime.' She tilted her head and pinned me with her wide green eyes, pupils narrowed to a slit. 'Now about that holiday . . .'

'I got fired.' I pushed myself from the doorway and stomped to the living room.

'You got *what*?' The cat leapt on to the sofa.

I collapsed into the cushions with a groan. Grandmother started to claw the armrest.

'Stop that.'

'I can't help it. I've a lot of nervous energy. No one from this family has *ever* been fired. The humiliation! Are you sure they said *fired*? Maybe they said *hired*?'

'I'm out of a job, Gran. They won't even give me a reference.'

'You got *shot*.' Grandmother sat up. 'Hand me the phone, let me speak to them.'

'Sure.' I dragged a trembling hand through my tangled hair. It was time for another painkiller and the distant growling in my ears was maddening. Perhaps I was going insane. 'The governors are bound to change their mind when I put my Gran on the line.'

I stood and limped to the kitchen. Painkiller, vodka. Nothing to remain sober for anyway and my whole body shook with the need for a buzz. Let's see if the ghostly growling could withstand half a bottle of Absolut.

'*Ivy Elizabeth Mann*!' Grandmother bounded on to the work surface and miaowed. 'Put that down!'

I ignored her and poured another shot.

'There's nothing less attractive than a drunk. And you're still technically a teenager. Your mother would kill you.'

'I'm over eighteen.' I glared at her before downing the vodka in one. I was feeling better already. 'Anyway, I don't think I ever saw you without a gin in your hand.' I sniffed and considered the bottle.

'By the time you came along, I was married to your grandfather. You try being married for fifty years *sober*.'

'No thanks.' I poured another, lengthened it with a coke and lurched back to the sofa.

No more vodka for a while. No more salmon either. I dug under the cushion for last night's chocolate. No more chocolate come to that. No more luxuries. What kind of job could I do now? And what if Ortega blocked everything else I tried? *Destroy my life* he said. What else was he planning?

My head fell back, and I stared at the ceiling. Grandmother

glowered at me, then jumped on to my lap. She kneaded my thighs for a while, curled into a ball and fell asleep.

'Good idea,' I muttered, but I carried on watching the shadows creep towards the pendant light.

I know what you're thinking, I used to like those books too, but I'm not half faerie (or however you spell it), nor am I a demon, an angel, the reincarnation of a knight of old or a princess from another world. Mum's a Body Shop consultant living in a bungalow in Birmingham and Dad enters crossword competitions. He's won a car, two holidays and a lot of kitchen appliances since their divorce.

I'm normal. So very normal. And now I'm unemployed. What could be more normal than that?

'I don't even like baked beans,' I muttered, and pressed the button on the remote control. The news flickered on and I sighed. As my fingers moved to change channel, I froze. There'd been another attack: ten kids killed in Birmingham. I closed my eyes briefly. Where was *their* security officer? Another John Wick wannabe no doubt.

There was a government representative offering her thoughts and prayers on one side of the screen. On the other a man in a black suit.

'The people have had enough,' he was saying. 'The Conservatives have let this situation spiral out of control. What is the Commission actually *doing* to prevent spellcasting on British soil? Anything? We need *change*. None of us is safe. Join us in a march outside Westminster on the 23rd April,' he shrilled. 'Demand a general election and vote for the British Republican Party. The BRP are the only ones who can save us.'

The door buzzer rang. I blinked at the drink in my hand. It was tilted towards my legs, the teetering liquid threatening Gran's fur.

The buzzer rang again. I didn't have any friends. At least, not ones who would be around this time of day. I *definitely* didn't want double glazing. Maybe it's an ambulance chaser. I sat up straighter and Gran sank a claw into my knee in warning.

I pictured a nice young woman at the door. 'Have you been injured at work?' She'd say.

'*Yes*, actually,' I muttered, and I shoved Gran on to a sofa cushion. She growled at me, turned around and went back to sleep.

The buzzer rang again, and I grabbed my crutch. 'Hang on,' I limped towards the door, vodka slopping over my wrist. 'Yes, I have been injured and no, it wasn't my fault.'

I looked at my hands for a moment, not sure how to work the handle. Both were in use. Finally, I leant the crutch against the wall, balanced on one foot and yanked the door open.

There was a goth on the doorstep.

5

'HELL, NO.' I tried to slam the door, but Norah stuck her foot in, blocking me. I was too drunk and off balance to force the issue. She pushed her way into the flat, eyes skimming every surface and recoiling at the mess. Of course, she was an *Ortega*, probably had servants. I grabbed my crutch again and hobbled after her. 'Out!' I gestured at the open door with the rubber bung on the end of my stick.

Norah shook her head. She had a thick bandage around her forehead, a slash of white striping the obsidian of her hair. Her eyes had dark rings and she had a very real pallor, nothing to do with make-up. Good, I hoped she had a killer headache.

In the background, the guy from the BRP was arguing with a government minister in strident tones.

'How did you find my address?' I glared.

Norah shrugged, her eyes still darting. She rubbed the back of her neck with one hand, the other clutched her rucksack.

'Get out,' I said, again.

She shook her head and let her eyes rest on my face. They were bloodshot and wide with fear. 'You have to help me,' she begged. 'I've nowhere else to go.'

'Ha!' I laughed bitterly and downed the rest of my flat vodka and coke. I had to do something with it. I tossed the empty glass on to the armchair. 'Ha,' I said, again. 'Out!'

'Please,' she followed the glass and sat down. 'I can't.' She glanced at the television, flinched, then reached out and pressed the power button on the remote. The argument blinked out.

I sighed. Norah was a goth. But she was also younger than me and I'd made a vow. Not a magical vow at midnight on the blood of my ancestors, just a promise to *myself* to help kids.

I kicked the door shut and stamped back to the living area, where I leant on the wall between the clock and the fireplace, massaging my aching heart. 'Well, what is it?'

Norah twisted the handle of her bag between her fingers. 'Can I . . . can I have a glass of water.'

'Sure.' I cocked my head towards the kitchen, and she followed my gaze, then she looked back down.

'Um, it's OK.'

Like I was going to serve her. I said I'd made a promise to help kids, not wait on an entitled would-be murderess. I folded my arms – the crutch dangled from my elbow.

Norah cleared her throat – once, twice. I made no sound of encouragement.

36

'I—I'm sorry you got hurt,' she said eventually, looking up at me with big eyes.

'Hurt I can deal with,' I growled. 'But you cost me my job.'

She jerked as if I'd poked her with my stick. 'Y—your job?'

'Your brother,' I said, and she swallowed.

'Oh . . . I see.' She hung her head. 'I—I'll speak to him.'

I leant closer to her, lifting my body from its support. 'Did you do it?' I curled a lip. 'Did you call those two hounds?'

There was a long silence and Norah's knuckles whitened over the sigils covering her bag. Then she nodded. It was a tiny movement, barely noticeable, but it was there. She'd done it.

'Tell your brother,' I snapped. 'Maybe I'll get my job back.'

'I can't,' Norah whispered. 'You don't understand.'

'I understand that you tried to murder—'

'N—no.' Norah leapt to her feet. 'I didn't know. I knew . . . something . . . but not that. As soon as I realised how awful it was going to be, I tried to prevent it.'

'But?'

The word hovered in the air between us, on dark wings.

'Y—you stopped it, and now . . .' She looked at her bag again. And I knew.

The knowledge dropped into my head as if I'd always known. 'I banished the first hound properly, but the *second* one just had the portal closed on it. It wasn't exorcised and so it's still out there.' I thumped onto a bar stool. 'It's still owed a life. And it's after yours – isn't it?'

Norah nodded. 'You owe me,' she said suddenly, and her face was set in hard lines that reminded me of her brother. '*You* stopped the spell and now one of them is after *me*. You owe me, and so you have to *help* me.' Her voice was arrogant, but her hands were shaking. 'I can *hear* it,' she whispered. 'Howling in the back of my head. It's hunting. C—coming for me.' A tear traced its way down her chin and on to her bag, blotching indigo ink. 'Help me!'

'Sod it!' I felt suddenly sober. Three vodkas and a painkiller gone, just like that. I could argue with her. I could send her away. But as I said, I'd made a vow and had to help Norah because, at the end of the day, everything that had happened to her, everything that was happening to all of them . . . was my fault.

✷ ✷ ✷

I hated to remember, but in my mind's eye it was already four years ago and I was sitting with the others in front of the old factory. Danny had built a small fire in a disposable barbeque and it flickered between us.

'To Violet,' Elena giggled, but she was crying too, and I wasn't sure whether to take the stolen Malibu off her or give her a hug. Danny solved the problem by wrapping one arm tightly around Elena.

I accepted the Malibu. I'd never tried alcohol before and didn't much like it; the stuff burned. To me it was like drinking hot tears, but that seemed right somehow. It was a special night: the anniversary of our best friend's death.

'To Violet.' I joined the toast and took a long swig, coughing as the alcohol mixed with memories and warmed my chest while filling me with new grief.

'And to the judge who sent the idiot down.' Danny took the Malibu.

'He didn't get long enough,' Elena snatched the bottle from him and sucked at it.

'What would have been?' I flicked a twig onto the fire. 'He got the maximum for a hit and run.'

'Life,' Elena spat. 'The death penalty?'

'Yeah, we could demand he gets extradited to America just so they can sit him in the chair.' Danny tightened his hug. 'He was a dumb kid, El. He'll live with it for the rest of his life.'

Elena wriggled from under his arm. 'Don't excuse him!'

'I'm not.' Danny frowned.

'It sounds like you're sorry for him!'

'I'm not, honestly.' Danny shook his blonde head. 'I'm just trying to find a way to live—'

'Well, don't.' Elena hurled the bottle and it smashed against the dirty brick wall behind us, splattering the remaining liquid in a wet chrysanthemum shape and leaving shards of white glass to glitter among the dead grass. She crawled to the other side of the fire. 'None of us should be – she can't.'

'I know you loved her, E,' Danny said, quietly. 'We all did.'

'Not like me.' Elena's tears shone on her face. She stared at me and her eyes were hollow. I shuddered. How had I not seen how damaged Vi's death had left her? 'How would you feel if it had been Ivy?'

Danny looked at me, a fast, hot glance and then away and back to Elena.

'Would you be able to "live with it", to "move on"?' Her words bit.

Danny shook his head and I tucked my hands under my armpits, suddenly cold.

'I—I brought this.' Elena picked up the messenger bag that she'd discarded by the fire. I leant forward, curious.

'I know it's stupid,' Elena pulled out a book. 'I know it is, but

. . . I want to do it. I want you to do it with me. You were her best friends.'

'What is it?' I scooted over to her side. The book was old, bound in dark leather and far bigger than a schoolbook. The name on the cover blurred, as alcohol and weed took their toll on my eyesight. 'Necro . . . what?'

'I got it from this shop when we were on holiday,' Elena stroked the cover soothingly, as if the book was a fractious child. 'You know how Mum loves those second-hand places.' She sniffed. 'I was looking through a pile of tat and there it was.' Elena opened the book and when I saw what was inside, my skin crawled. Swirls of text, written in dark red ink, scrawled and curled over the page like the ramblings of a lunatic. Over some of the words blotches could have been from a broken ink pen, tear marks or something . . . else. The whole thing screamed 'wrong'.

Danny leant over my shoulder. 'Creepy.'

'It's a spell book,' Elena said, and she flushed.

'How can you read that?' Danny put a finger on the page, then pulled back and wiped the tip on his shirt. 'It's not even English.'

'It's Latin I think . . . mainly Latin.' Elena hugged the book to her. 'I've done my research, OK. There's a spell in here. It's meant to . . .' she tailed off.

'Meant to what?' I shifted, uncomfortable. Somewhere an owl hooted, and I heard the distant clack and clatter of a train going over the old bridge. Dust shook and settled around us. Danny put a hand on my shoulder and I leant into him.

Elena met my eyes. 'It's meant to raise the dead.'

I looked up at Danny. He was licking his lips. Lips I'd been kissing only a couple of hours earlier. We'd stopped when Elena had arrived. It seemed cruel to remind her she'd never be kissing Vi again.

'I know it's stupid,' Elena was saying. 'I know it won't work – I'm not thick. I just thought . . . today it's . . . something.'

'Sure, of course we'll do it.' Danny squeezed my shoulder and I nodded.

'What do we have to do?'

6

THE CEMETERY WAS damp, the grass wet underfoot and grey in the darkness. Rustling amongst the graves made us cluster together, even though we knew it was likely nothing more than a fox or a hunting cat. Nevertheless, we were fifteen-years old, drunk and clinging to one another, terrified of our own daring. Elena held the book to her chest; I carried her messenger bag over one shoulder. There was weight to it – it still wasn't empty. I wondered what else she had brought.

I was holding Danny's hand, enjoying the familiarity of his palm flat against my own, his fingers entwined in mine. He was always growing, his hands bigger than mine but still those of a boy. He had developed a stoop recently, as if he was ashamed of his new tallness, and he ducked a little as he looked at the world through his thick fringe. I wondered how it would feel to hold him when he was a man, when he had the confidence of his height and breadth. His hand would probably envelop mine. I held him a little tighter as we stepped amongst the dead.

The graves had no uniformity to them, like the mouth of a tramp who'd never seen a dentist. Some were small enough to trip us while others towered or leaned, the crumbling stone moss-slicked and impossible to read. Violet's stood higher than the others, made from white marble with lettering still crisp-edged and fresh bunches of flowers laid at the foot, dying in their damp wrappings.

We stopped and I stared at her name *Violet Dawn Adams*. I remembered how she used to write it on her textbooks with such long swirls, it was almost calligraphic. She went through a phase of making the lines of the V into the stems of roses. Her artist's fingers drawing each petal with infinite care.

Suddenly, I couldn't breathe with how much I missed her. Danny pulled me into a hug. He looked at Elena. 'What do we do, E?'

Elena pulled her pale hair forward, dragging her ponytail down over one shoulder. She took a deep breath. Then she laid the open book on top of Vi's grave, smoothing the pages as a gust of wind tried to flap them like the wings of a bird.

'I need the bag.' She gestured to me and I pulled it over my head, tangling the strap in my own brown hair. Elena took it and I watched her remove four candles and a compass.

She consulted the compass and placed the first candle just to the left of Violet's headstone.

'Here,' she handed the other three to Danny. 'That one's North, we need them around the grave, one at South, one East and one West.'

'Got it.' Danny flashed me a nervous grin and set out the candles in a cross shape. Next Elena produced four small glasses and a bottle of Evian.

'One at the base of each candle.' She filled a glass and handed it to me, which I took with trembling fingers. 'Go on.'

'R—right.' I laid them out on the bumpy ground, careful not to spill and trying not to think about Elena's corpse mouldering below us. I'd heard that hair and nails kept growing when you died. Was she nothing now but a skeleton in a blue dress, wrapped in faded red curls, her nails like claws? Or did flesh still cling to her bones? I covered my mouth.

Finally, Elena took out a little bowl that shone with a copper glow in the light of the half moon, and a pair of nail scissors. She handed Danny the bowl, then clipped a hank of her hair from her ponytail. 'Now you.' She stepped to my side, grabbed my hair and before I could protest that it would ruin my blunt cut, she cut a chunk out. She tossed our hair into the bowl, then reached up, caught Danny's fringe and sliced some of his to add to the mix. The strands mingled: brown, blonde and almost white. She pulled the lighter we'd used for the joint out of her pocket and lit the soft fuzz. Instantly the air stank as the hair curled up, turned brown and disintegrated. She put the bowl in the centre of the candles.

'Now, we need a circle of earth,' she said, almost prayerfully. I glanced at Danny and he shrugged. We knelt in the darkness, humping damp mud between our palms, our knees in the dirt – working our way around the candles as Elena lit them, coaxing flickering flames into life.

'This isn't going to work, is it?' I whispered to Danny as we met again.

He nudged me. 'Course not – it might make E feel better, that's all. It's a way of saying goodbye. She wasn't welcome at the funeral, remember?'

'Vi's mum is a bigot,' I snapped. 'She loved Elena.'

'I know.'

We stepped over the circle of raised earth and joined Elena, putting our arms around her. 'Are you OK, E?' I asked.

Elena nodded. She was flushed; even in the gloom I could see her cheeks darken as she looked at the book in front of the copper bowl. Candlelight reflected from its polished surface.

'Are you sure you want to do this?' I murmured.

Elena simply raised her hands. 'You have to repeat after me,' she said, without looking at me.

'OK.' I felt suddenly sober and a chill shrank me into my jacket. 'I guess.'

Moonlight speared the cloud and the air shimmered in front of us.

'From cloud to sea,' Elena said, and she looked meaningfully at Danny.

'From cloud to sea,' we chanted, our voices blending.

'From crown to throne. From blood to bough, from skin to bone.'

I repeated after her, but it was almost as if I didn't need to – the words flowed from my tongue as though I'd always known them.

'From tree to root, from earth to sky, come now, make her death a lie.'

My voice had almost caught up with Elena's. Danny's deeper tones burred under ours, like a song. I couldn't have stopped if I had wanted to.

'*For thou who sleeps in stone and clay, heed our call and rise this day. Enter through the mortal door, assemble flesh and walk once more.*'

Elena's voice rose to a scream.

'*Quondam multo ambulant!*'

Around us the wind started to rise, lifting my hair over my shoulders and whirling leaves and twigs in a tornado that left the book and its sacrifice of burned hair oddly still.

'*Quondam multo ambulant!*'

I grabbed Danny, digging my fingers into his shoulder. He was tense, his muscles taut under his shirt; it was like clutching a rock. His own hair blew over his eyes, snatching them from me.

'*Quondam multo ambulant!*'

The candles blew out and the wind died as if it had never been. There was silence.

A cloud scudded across the bright sliver of the new moon and darkness rolled around us.

I laughed, awkwardly, and tried to smooth my hair. My arms were stippled with goosebumps. Elena stood still, her hands dangling limply at her sides.

'E?' I cleared my throat and tried again. 'E?'

'Are you all right?' Danny stepped forward. 'You didn't really expect—'

Elena shook her head and said nothing. She stared at the gentle mound beneath her feet, her shoulders silently shaking. I took her hand. Tears dripped from her nose. I watched a heavy, salt-soaked droplet teeter on the end of her chin then drop through the air, elongating before it splatted into the ash-filled copper bowl.

I raised my head. 'Dann—'

The earth exploded.

I was thrown one way and Elena the other. My shoulder slammed hard enough against a gravestone that I heard it creak and grit rattled against my collarbone. Pain blinded me for a moment, and I grabbed my arm, sure it was broken. When I could see again, I stared, unable to believe it. Violet was crouching in the centre of the tipped-over candles – her long hair tangled like brambles, her skin grey and peeling. Her dress was a threadbare shroud with holes barely held together by torn threads. Between the shreds I could see bare muscle and sinew, yellowing bone. One side of her face was collapsed inwards and I cringed as I realised that I could see her teeth through her cheek.

'V—Violet?' Elena's voice trembled in the air. Beneath Vi's bloodied feet there were splinters of coffin.

Danny was still on his feet, balanced inside the circle of earth with arms outstretched. He stared, frozen and shocked. Violet ignored Elena – instead she turned to Danny, her mouth open, in a tortured shriek that made no sound. She had no voice – it had rotted away.

She rose and staggered forward.

Instinctively, Danny put his arms out to catch her. 'Vio—'

She tore out his throat.

I screamed.

I screamed as his blood splattered my face and splashed my arms and legs. I screamed as he collapsed to his knees, his eyes seeking mine with a terrified *'why?'* I screamed as his fingers, the fingers of the hands I would never see grow into a man's after all, groped for the wound, trying to hold it closed. I screamed as he fell forward, his cheek hitting the dirt. I screamed as his legs twitched and one hand reached for mine. Then, as he went still, the

47

light in his eyes dying and blood matting in his hair . . . I screamed.

Violet lurched towards the sound of my voice but came up against the raised circle of mud as if it was a wall. She pressed against it, her bloodied nails slashing for me as though she needed my scream for herself. I scrabbled backwards and pressed myself against the grave. My breath hitched in my throat.

'Violet, it's all right, you didn't mean it.' Elena was crawling towards her. 'It'll be OK.,' She was reaching for her girlfriend with shaking hands.

'Stay out of the circle!' I gasped. 'Don't go in.' I scrabbled around desperate for something, a weapon . . . anything. My fingers closed around the shape of the lighter, thrown from Elena's pocket.

It was all I had. I tore my eyes from Danny's and flicked the lighter on. The tiny flame caught instantly and lit the darkness. I was crying for Danny, I knew that, but in a distant way. The horror had wrapped its arms around me, muffling everything. I leant forward.

'What are you *doing*?' Elena howled. My arm crossed the line of earth and I held the flame to the tinder-dry rags that framed Vi's skeletal legs. They began to burn as if oiled.

In a way, I suppose they were – fat had soaked into them as she had rotted and now it lit her like a firework.

Violet spun as the flames ate at her, her shriek still unvoiced.

She reached for Elena, no recognition in those blank eyes. I scuttled backwards once more, retreating to the safety of the grave. There I covered my face and watched between my fingers, like a child, as what was left of my best friend fragmented. Flakes of ash lifted into the night and merged with the stars.

When the remains fell to the ground, smashing into the shards of the coffin, Elena wailed as if her heart had been ripped out. My own chest was as hollow as the copper bowl that lay upturned between us.

Vi stopped moving and Elena lurched to her feet. She stared at me, her face tortured and pale. Then she turned and ran.

✳ ✳ ✳

The police came. I honestly don't know what I told them, but they didn't believe me. They believed I'd been drinking though. I think they thought we'd been involved in a hazing ritual of some sort which had gone terribly wrong. I was in shock, and a minor, and my dad took me to hospital.

Policemen stood outside my door for three days while I lay and stared at the ceiling, thought about Danny and waited for Elena. There was talk of a trial.

Then everything changed.

7

THE CRAZY THING is, I honestly don't know what happened.
Nothing about what we did should have worked. In those
days, magic wasn't real. You couldn't raise the dead – never mind
what language your rhyme was in, or how much hair you shaved
off your head. Elena, Danny and I should have had a laugh and a
cry, then gone home to wake up with hangovers.

You may be wondering why the police let me go? It was because
they realised I was telling the truth. Suddenly there were hell
beasts coming out of the walls. In some cases, literally. I was what
you might call, patient zero – my experience only the first. Spells
conducted by wiccans, incantations read off the internet, chants
recited by D&D nerds – they'd started to work, and it was chaos.

After the initial flurry of excitement, law-abiding citizens realised how dangerous the whole thing was. Treating spells the same way they would semi-automatic rifles, most adults refused to even look at them. I guess the problem would have been much more serious outside the UK (I mean, can you imagine if this had happened in America?), but it seemed that the effect operated in a radius, with Violet's grave at the centre of the circle, weakening as it grew further from London. Once past the UK coastline, you could barely raise a hell bunny, let alone a hell hound.

Luckily, for some reason, most of those who did think about using a demon from the dark realms to off the tax man, just didn't have the juice. Spells don't work well for grown-ups. Perhaps they lack imagination or passion. I don't know. There's something about teenagers and magic. Maybe it's hormones.

The problem is that teenagers are the most volatile breed on the planet. A teenage girl and a spell book; that's a more terrifying combination than Vlad III and a hot spike.

But *why*? That's the question that was never truly answered. I was interviewed until I thought my ears would bleed – asked the same questions over-and-over by police, psychologists, university professors, two bishops and, towards the end, a trio of wiccans and a psychic.

The pressure got to Mum.

Dad stayed, at least for a while, but she struggled. Every time the news reported a magic-induced injury, her eyes scorched me. Every time there was a knock at the door and some suit stood there with more questions, she pulled further away. I'd always been Daddy's girl anyway, I suppose.

Then there was an incident involving her niece and a possession spell. She said she was only going to her sister's for a few weeks, just until the funeral was over and Maggie was back on her feet.

She moved into a flat in Birmingham a couple of months later. She'd always liked the buzz of the city, but she couldn't face London, or me, any more.

Dad stayed until I was eighteen. I hadn't been allowed to go back to school – the other parents saw my face in the paper and put two and two together. They campaigned tirelessly to keep me away from their children and so he home-schooled me, trying hopelessly to get me to pass an A-level.

It was living with his dead mother that sent him over the edge, I think. He buried himself in crosswords after Gran arrived and a week after my birthday he moved – apologetically – to Sutton Coldfield to be nearer Mum. We still speak about once a week and every so often he sends me kitchen appliances. I usually sell them.

Now I'm alone, except for Gran (which is another story). The suits concluded that somehow Danny, Elena and I had managed to make the right noises, in the right place, at a time when walls between realities were thin. They used the words quantum and dimensions; they talked about resonation and relativity. They all used different language, but it boiled down to this: we'd created a rift. Dark matter was now entering our world and manifesting as dark magic.

Hell on Earth.

And so *that's* why I work as a security guard in my old school, trying to protect the children I'd endangered. It's why I vowed to help kids like Norah, why I have no friends and why I remain as single as if I'm the last of my own species. Because the whole thing is *my fault*.

Don't ask me how Elena feels about it all – by the time I got out of custody her parents had moved the family away and slapped their house on the market. I never saw her again.

Gran, in case you were wondering, was the result of a later attempt to close the rift. The suits thought that getting one of the original players (me) to repeat a version of the first spell might just shut the whole thing down. There was no Violet but they exhumed Gran, thinking my affinity to her might negate the fact that Elena and Danny were both gone. By the time I agreed to risk it, I was probably too old and so instead of raising the dead, all I managed was to trap poor Gran's soul in the body of a nearby tabby. The rift remained open. She still hasn't forgiven me.

✳ ✳ ✳

I opened my eyes. Well, that was a nasty journey into my own past. Thanks Norah. Now the girl sat staring at me with eyes like those of a drowning puppy. 'You're going to help me, right?'

I knocked my head against the wall and groaned for good measure. 'Sure,' I sighed. 'I'll help you. But I need the book. I need the *Necronomicon*.'

Norah swallowed and gazed at her hands. 'I don't have it any more.' She looked up quickly. 'But I can get it.'

'Get it then.' I replied, pointing to the door.

Norah stood, just as Gran chose to wake up. She stretched and mewed, looked a little startled at herself, and then glared at our visitor. 'Who are you?'

Norah backed away so fast she tripped on her own boots. 'I—I'll come back.' She swung her bag over her shoulder and raced for the hallway.

'If I'd have known that would happen,' I said glowering at Gran, 'I'd have had you chase her off when she arrived.'

Gran stretched again, farted and leapt on to the windowsill. She put a paw on the window and watched the forlorn figure race down the street. Then her ears twitched.

'Ivy,' she mewed. 'Ivy, quick.'

'What is it? I can't *be* quick.' I hobbled to the window and stood next to Gran, my ears shivering with the faintest tinnitus snarl. 'What did you see?'

Gran looked up at me, her pupils so narrow they were hardly visible. 'It was Danny,' she said. 'That boy you used to kiss. I saw him.'

I stiffened. 'No, Gran,' I dug my fingers into her soft fur. 'Danny's been dead almost five years.'

'I know what I saw,' Gran clawed at the glass until it squeaked. 'And I saw that boy.'

'You're seeing things.' I lifted her by her fat stomach and hauled her on to the floor as she tried to sandbag on me. 'Or maybe it was someone who looked like Danny. It's been a long time.' I cleared my throat. 'There must be a lot of blonde boys . . .'

Gran's tail shot into the air, fluffing like a toilet brush, and she stalked past me to the kitchen. 'I *know* what I saw,' she growled. 'Now feed me!'

✳ ✳ ✳

It was three hours before my door shook with the sound of the buzzer. I took a deep breath and opened it. I'd been wracking my brain, trying to think of a way that I could save Norah Ortega. I was beginning to worry that there wasn't one. But it had been a long time since I'd seen that book and I wasn't a naïve kid any more. Perhaps I could find some way to help.

She was clutching her bag in both arms, her face pale. 'Quick,' she shoved the bag at me, making me teeter on my crutches. 'Take it.'

She raced past me, as if there was someone in the hall behind her. I looked up and down the corridor. There was nothing to see but the cigarette-stained carpet and a horrible Monet print that almost covered the marks on the wall left when Sami and Arun Patel accidentally raised three ghouls which had already eaten their mother by the time I got home and heard the screams. At the far end, stairs wound up to the second floor. The light was broken. It flickered on, off, on, off, sending the stairwell first into pitch darkness and then lurid glare; there was a faint buzzing from the struggling bulb. I suppose it *was* a little creepy. I shrugged and closed my door.

Norah was in the kitchen, drinking a glass of water and watching Gran with suspicious eyes.

'Gran, this is Norah.' I hefted the bag on to the table. 'Norah, Gran.'

'Gran?' Norah edged out of the kitchen, staying as far away from the fat tabby as the walls allowed. Gran rolled over dismissively and started to lick her butt clean. I wasn't sure I'd ever get used to seeing that. Dad certainly couldn't.

'Long story,' I said, opening her bag. 'Let's see it then.'

The book was just as I remembered it, if a little more battered. I stared at it balefully and it was almost as if it was glaring back at me. My fingertips hovered over the cover.

'Where did you get this?' I whispered. I tried to think about what Norah's brother had said – that there had to be more than one copy – but I knew this was the original, *the* book Elena had brought to us that night. I had learnt not to ignore my instincts. What did it mean that it had come back to me?

Norah flinched and I tore my gaze away from the now-familiar title scrawled across the brittle leather to see her shivering. I frowned. 'You can still hear the hound?'

'You can't?' She dug bitten nails into her palms.

'It's getting closer?'

'Louder. Closer.' She closed her eyes. 'I—I don't think my protection spell is working any more. It's as though it's just at the end of the road.'

I nodded. 'It's got the scent of your spirit now. End of the road I can cope with, let me know when it sounds like it's in the building.'

Norah made a sound that was half-agreement, half-sob and I hardened my heart. She didn't have time for me to baby her. 'Sit.' I gestured to my single dining chair. The table had come with only two and one was in my bedroom being used as a wardrobe.

'Before I look at the book, tell me – what were you trying to do with it?'

Norah stared at me with wet eyes, then she fumbled in her pocket and pulled out her wallet. She opened it and I thought for a moment she was going to offer me money, but instead she slid out a picture – the one I'd seen before of a little girl in pigtails.

'My sister,' she said, as if that explained it all.

I took the photo from her, careful to handle only the edges. The girl was standing in a park, swings at her back – she had one hand on her hip and was twisted half away from the camera. A beaming smile, utterly unforced, showed two missing front teeth and her hair was in lopsided pigtails.

'That was the last picture she had with hair,' Norah said hoarsely. 'She lost it all . . .' she stopped talking and I understood.

'When did she die?'

Norah sniffed and wiped her nose with her palm, upwards, like a kid herself. 'It's been almost a year.' She hunched in the chair, haunted. 'Her name was Natalie.' She looked up at me, her eyes wild. 'It isn't fair. She was *nine*.' She leapt to her feet, as if I'd said otherwise. 'She was a kid, and a *good* kid, y'know. Not like me or Nicky. She was always bringing home injured animals or asking to take food out to someone on the street. She never did anything wrong.'

'You mean she didn't deserve it,' I said gently. 'No one does.' Violet and Danny's faces flashed in front of me and I pushed them away.

'*She* didn't. I would've understood if it had been me, or, or—'

'Nicky, right?' Nicholas Ortega. I tried not to sneer as I said his name. 'That's not how it works though.'

Norah started to pace, walking away from the book on the table. Gran scrambled on to the sofa and miaowed at her, offering her head. Norah froze, then tentatively put out a finger and touched Gran's ear. Gran butted her hand. Norah stiffened, but scratched Gran's chin and then ran her palm down her back, ending at her tail. Gran made a satisfied sound and looked at me.

'All right,' I snapped. 'I'm doing what I can.' I looked at the book again. 'You wanted to raise the dead.' It had to be the same spell. 'You know that doesn't work – she would have come back as a revenant. No soul, no spark.'

Norah shook her head. 'That's not what they said. They said the spell to raise Nat *would* work if I provided blood . . . innocent blood.' She avoided my gaze.

I thought back to the graveyard. Would Vi have come back as *Violet*, if we'd cut our skin rather than our hair? Would Gran have been properly raised? I refused to believe it. 'You told me she was a good person. You can't think she'd have wanted that.' I couldn't help my barbed tone. In my defence, it had been a long time since I'd spoken properly with a real person.

Norah glared. 'I don't care. Her death wasn't fair. But . . . I didn't think it would be like . . . like it was.'

'What *did* you think?'

'I don't know, OK. They didn't say it would be s—so awful'

'Hang on.' Looking at the book had distracted me. My head jerked up. 'You said *they*?'

Norah opened her mouth just as my metal door lock, complete with a huge chunk of wood, smacked into my injured shoulder as the door crashed into the wall. The sound, like falling masonry, made Gran jump upwards with a wail, rigid and terrified.

Norah yelped too and I spun around to see my doorway filled with the dark fury that was Nicholas Ortega. He strode forward wrathfully, his dark hair speckled with dust from my door frame.

'What are you doing with my sister?' He roared.

8

I SLUNG THE BOOK and rucksack under the sofa and, abandoning my crutch, hobble-ran as best I could to the bedroom. I kept Matilda by my bed, in case of night-time intruders. Why hadn't I fetched her after Norah had gone for the book? Idiot.

My thigh burned and I felt stitches pop, but I didn't slow down. I dodged the hall table, hearing a yell and crash behind me as Ortega slammed into it. It really does stick out further than you think. It gave me time to reach the room before he did, and I was glad I'd never listened to Gran and moved it somewhere more sensible.

As Norah shouted in the background, I slammed the door on 'Nicky's' reaching hand and heard him curse as I threw myself across the bed. My fingers closed over Matilda and I rolled, coming up to face him as he burst into the bedroom. Gran was hanging from one of his thighs, like a sporran, her claws deep in his leg. I grinned maniacally. 'Go, Gran!'

He was holding his, presumably bruised, left leg with one hand; with the other he was trying to yank Gran free. She was having none of it.

'Stop it!' I snapped. I stood swaying on my bleeding leg, the machete dancing in the air between us. 'Gran, let go of him before he hurts you.'

Gran hissed one last time, then sheathed her claws and dropped silently to the floor. She stalked to my side, glaring like a policeman forced to abandon the arrest of a lifetime. Ortega stared at her.

'Back up,' I gasped at him. Gran miaowed agreement.

Slowly he raised his hands and retreated towards the living room. Gran and I followed.

'You can't imagine I'm going to leave my sister here,' he said, as if his presence in my small flat was not only reasonable but that I was being ridiculous in thinking it otherwise.

'Get out of my home,' I said, low and quiet. 'You aren't welcome.'

'Fine by me.' He looked over his shoulder. 'Get the book, Norah, we're leaving.' He rubbed his leg again, the angry expression darkening his face still further.

Norah pulled the book out from under the sofa, edged across the room and stepped between us. She was trembling. 'Stop it, Nicky, please!' she said. 'I'm not going anywhere.'

Ortega grabbed her by one elbow and Norah blenched. He started to pull her towards the door. 'Let's go!'

Gran growled a warning and Norah wriggled, frantically, her

eyes pinned to the broken doorway. Eventually her terror shattered her brother's determination. With a grunt, he let her go and she hugged the book to her chest as she backed towards me and away from the door.

'What have you done to her?' Ortega pulled a sleek phone from his jacket. 'I'm calling Andrews.'

'No!' Norah reached me and stood her ground. 'I need to be here, Nicky. I need *her*. She's the only one who can help me.'

'I'm sure that's what she told you,' said Ortega, dragging a hand impatiently through his hair, 'but it's not true. Give me the book and we can—'

'We can what?' Norah yelled. 'You *had* the book. You haven't even looked at it.'

'I haven't had—'

'Time, right. I *know*.' Norah looked past her brother, once more staring at the door, her eyes blank with terror.

'It's in the building, isn't it?' I gasped with sudden understanding. 'It's coming *now*?'

She nodded, the tiniest movement of her head, and I shoved her behind me. The hound wouldn't manifest like it had in the school – there was no spell calling it, so we wouldn't even see it – but it would take Norah, just the same. They were connected. I shook my head as my tinnitus increased to almost deafening levels.

'Hide, Gran,' I rasped. I didn't know what the hound would do if it came across a cat, even if it *was* a possessed one. It *was* still a dog, after all. Gran spat, flexed her claws and belly-slid under the sofa.

'It's disgusting under here,' she muttered.

'What the blazes is going on?' Ortega shouted, and the carpet in the doorway depressed as if something very heavy had just trodden on it.

'Get away from the door,' I yelled, rubbing my ear.

'N—Nicky—' Norah reached a hand for him, but the carpet depressed on either side of him as if something large had simply walked through his body.

Ortega shuddered, 'What the hell . . .'

'That's right, now shut up,' I was counting. Judging by the paw prints sizzling on my rug, the hound could have had Norah by now but it was playing with its food. 'Bad doggie!' I muttered. It was circling us. I turned, keeping Norah at my back, holding Matilda out in front and praying the blade would make the hound hesitate. My gear was under the kitchen sink. I know, not a great place but it's not exactly valuable and I can't wear it twenty-four seven. Hell hounds aren't exactly common visitors to the flat.

Ortega folded his arms. 'I don't know what kind of game this is . . .'

'Shut up!' I was watching for footsteps. 'If you want your sister to live, you'll throw me my kit. It's under the kitchen sink.'

He stared. 'What are you *talking* about?'

'Under the sink, hurry!'

'Nicky, *please*!' Norah was sobbing now.

Ortega hesitated, but his sister's tears broke him. He raced for the kitchen. I kept one eye on him as he ducked his head under the sink and came up with my belt. 'This?'

'Throw it!'

He hurled it underarm and I caught it with my free hand. The bell tinkled merrily. But there was no time for a full ritual and I had none of the hound's blood anyway, so I couldn't exorcise it. There was only one thing I could do for Norah right now.

I shook the Bible on to the floor, tossed the belt to one side and kicked open the book. Behind me Norah was breathing in short, desperate pants, as if she was too terrified to scream. I wondered if she could see the hound, or just hear it. Was it growling, or staying silent?

'Read, Norah!' I yelled.

Norah grabbed my shoulder. 'Are you su—'

'Do it!' I pushed her to her knees. Norah gasped and her eyes fell on the Bible. A whole section was underlined.

I hadn't kicked it open randomly. That book had spent long hours pressed open to a certain page. My way of making sure that, left to itself, it would fall open at the place *I* wanted it to. The Lord helps those who help themselves, that's what Gran always says.

A footprint appeared barely an arm's-length from my right foot. I lunged with Matilda, but my blade met nothing but air.

'Read!' I yelled, trying not to picture what she would look like when the hound tore into her. Would it have to manifest to do that, or would it be able to tear her apart invisibly? Would we just see Norah disintegrate into bloody pieces in front of us?

Stumbling over the words, she read. '*I—I sought the Lord, and he answered me; he delivered me from all my fears.*'

The footprint forming by my side, lifted – as if the hound had hesitated to put down its full weight.

'Keep going.' I thrust again with Matilda. This time it seemed there was some resistance, as though I'd dragged the blade through water.

Norah nodded. I looked up. Her brother was still in the kitchen, armed now with my carving knife and fork like the host of a psycho dinner party.

'*Th—those who look to him are radiant,*' Norah read. '*th—their faces are never covered with shame. This poor man called, and the Lord heard him; he saved him out of all his troubles. The angel of the Lord encamps around those who fear him, and he delivers them.*'

She glanced at me, white-faced. 'I—I think it's working.'

I nodded and did another sweep with Matilda. This time there was greater resistance and I stumbled when I pulled the blade free.

'*Taste and see that the Lord is good; blessed is the one who takes refuge in him. Fear the Lord, you his holy people, for those who fear him lack nothing.*' She glanced up again. 'It's angry.' Tears were trickling down her cheeks.

'Don't stop reading, Norah.' I looked around wildly for indented carpet. Thank goodness I'd listened to Gran and invested in a thick rug – if I still had bare floorboards, the hound would be invisible.

'*Th—the lions may grow weak and hungry, but those who seek the Lord lack n—no good thing.*' She put her hands over her ears, and I waved Matilda around us. I still heard nothing, but a footstep appeared further away from us. The hound was retreating.

'*Come, my children, listen to me;*' Norah cried. '*I will teach you the fear of the Lord. Whoever of you loves life and desires to see many good days, keep your tongue from evil and your lips from telling lies. Turn from evil and do good; seek peace and pursue it. The eyes of the Lord are on the righteous, and his ears are attentive to their cry.*'

She sobbed as she read, and her hands trembled over her head. '*Th—the face of the Lord is against those who do evil, to blot out their name from the Earth.*'

My voice blended with hers: '*The righteous cry out, and the Lord hears them; he delivers them from all their troubles.*' Norah stopped reading but I carried on, knowing the verses from memory. '*The*

Lord is close to the broken-hearted and saves those who are crushed in spirit. The righteous person may have many troubles, but the Lord delivers him from them all; he protects all his bones, not one of them will be broken. Evil will slay the wicked; the foes of the righteous will be condemned. The Lord will rescue his servants; no one who takes refuge in him will be condemned!' I screamed the last line and Norah huddled at my feet. There was a growl that reverberated through the whole apartment and then a sudden feeling of emptiness.

I touched my own ear; my tinnitus had suddenly vanished. My heart sank. What kind of tinnitus could be banished by Psalm 34? A problem for another time.

'Is it gone?' I looked at Norah. She peered out from behind her hair and then nodded.

'What the devil just happened?' Ortega strode forward, brandishing my carving set. I ignored him.

'It's a sticking plaster; it won't last.' I pulled Norah to her feet and sheathed Matilda. 'We scared it away, but it'll be back. It might not be alone next time, and those words aren't strong enough to ward it off again. We have to get to hallowed ground until I can work out what to do about this.'

I glanced at the sofa. There was a strong smell of cat pee. I sighed.

'More than one *what*?' Ortega blocked the way to the door. 'What kind of trick is this? It's money you're after, isn't it? If you think you can frighten my sister and get money out of her, you're very much mistaken. The police will be dealing with you.' He slammed my carving set down on the hall table, making it shudder.

I was already picking my belt up and strapping it on. 'That was a hell hound, Ortega.' I pulled my flak vest down from its hook behind the door and slid my arms inside. 'Your sister *did* call it and because it was sent back hungry, rather than being properly exorcised, it's after her now. Clear?' I clipped the vest closed.

Ortega's arms dropped to his sides. 'You *did* call them?'

Norah flushed.

'But you were home all night.'

'Oh *please*,' I snapped. 'Like a teenager can't get out of her house without her older brother knowing. Let me guess, you work late a *lot*?' I grunted as I bent to pick up my crutch, I settled it into the crook of my arm as the bell at my belt tinkled. I opened the broken door, looking regretfully at the smashed lock. 'You'll be paying for that to be fixed. If anything gets nicked while we're out, you're paying for that too.' I jerked my head at Norah. 'Come on, we've got to go.' I watched her scuttle past, head down. 'And we'll be talking about my job,' I snapped, as Ortega followed her.

Ortega looked only at his sister, his brown eyes were wide and hurt. He caught her elbow. 'Why, Norah?'

They stood in the hallway, under the flickering light with the stained wall as background.

'I had to,' Norah said, with tears in her eyes. 'Don't you understand? I had to do it . . . to bring Natalie back.'

'Natalie?' To my intense satisfaction, Ortega looked as if he had been smacked in the face with a shovel. He groped his way to the wall, then along it to the stairs. He collapsed on the bottom tread with his head in his hands, looking suddenly much more human. There was a muffled shout from the flat upstairs. We ignored it. 'Norah, you can't bring Natalie back,' he said into his palms. 'You think I didn't look into it first thing? It's never been done.'

'He's right.' I touched Norah's shoulder. She was vibrating with tension. 'It's never been done successfully. Your sister would have come back as a revenant, or . . .' I looked back at the flat. 'You've met Gran. I think you can bring back the body *or* the spirit, not both.'

'That's not what *they* said.' She folded her arms. 'You didn't use innocent blood when you did the spell on your gran did you?'

'Obviously not,' I glowered. 'Because I know killing one person to save another isn't right, it doesn't matter how unfair you think their death is.'

Nicholas was faster on the uptake than I had been. His head snapped up. 'Norah, *who* said you should do this? Where did you get the book from?'

I nodded. 'There's no way that was just lying around. I *know* that book.'

Norah flushed. 'I—I can't tell you.'

Nicholas unfolded, jerked to his feet and grabbed her arm. 'You'll tell us.' He gave her a shake and her mouth set in a stubborn line.

'I thought you wanted me to help you?' I said as I started towards the main entrance to the flats. My leg ached like Gran had been clawing at it. I wished I could take more painkillers. 'I can't help you if you don't tell me.' I turned back with my hand on the door.

Norah clutched her bag to her chest and shook her head violently. Her brother's face twisted, and he opened his mouth to shout.

I spoke first. 'What did they make you swear on?'

Norah snivelled gratefully. 'N—Natalie's soul. They said if I tell, something will happen to it. Is that true?'

'Possibly.' There was something uncomfortable in my vest –

something edged, digging into my armpit. As I opened the door and light from the low sun flooded over us, I wriggled it out. It was the card I'd found in Norah's bag and pocketed: *Emporium*. Her eyes flashed to the card, then to me, and I knew.

'What's that?' Nicholas craned to see.

I held it up. 'I'm not sure, but I'm willing to bet it's where Norah got the book.'

Nicholas nodded grimly. 'Now I'm calling Andrews.'

9

ANDREWS TURNED OUT to be the Ortega family's personal driver. I stared at the man's muscles, bulging under his navy suit, and the wire running from one ear. There was no way they expected me to believe Andrews was only a chauffeur.

The light glinted from his shaved head and the hand that held the car door open for me was scarred. This was no mindless thug though, he remained silent, but his eyes glimmered.

'And Alfred was just a butler,' I muttered. Andrews offered a tight smile and said nothing.

The back of the limo was big enough for us to sit facing one another, with my leg stretched out in front of me. Ortega shifted so that there was no chance of his own thigh brushing mine and handed Norah a cola. 'Drink that, you look awful.'

She glowered at him but took the drink.

Surreptitiously I stroked the leather seat. It was as soft as Gran. The engine purred under me as Andrews brought it to life.

'Where are we going?' Nicholas asked. Norah shook her head and bit her lip.

I looked again at the card. 'It *has* to have contact details on it.' I turned it over in my fingers. 'It wouldn't be much of a business card otherwise.'

Nicholas leant forward. 'Andrews, we need to get moving. Pick a direction and go.'

The car slipped forward so smoothly I thought for a moment that it was my flat that had started to move. A fraction of the tension bled from Norah's face, the tightness around her eyes easing. Her shoulders slumped.

'That quietened it?' I asked.

'A little. I don't think it can keep up.'

I rubbed my head wearily. 'Sadly, we can't drive around forever. If you won't tell us about Emporium, we need to get you to hallowed ground.'

'Agreed.' Ortega leant forward, looking properly at me for the first time. 'Are you all right? You look—'

'Like I've been shot, sacked and fought three hell hounds?' I snapped. I shifted and my thigh left a bloody stain on the pale leather. 'Oh no, sorry!'

'Don't worry about it,' he said quickly.

But Norah handed me a cloth, pulled from a pocket in the seat that I hadn't even seen, and I put it under me, trying not to feel like a dog that had just messed on the carpet.

'Do we need to get you to a hospital?' Ortega said, but his tone

70

told me the answer had better be no.

I ground my teeth. 'Let's get Norah safe first.' I sensed his silent approval as I turned and rapped on the privacy screen. There was no response.

I started to knock again, and Ortega touched my shoulder. His hand was surprisingly warm. I twisted back and he pointed to a button. 'Press that and speak,' he said, so I pushed the button.

'Go right on Montgomery Street, then left at the roundabout.'

'You want to go to the Catholic cemetery.' The disembodied voice floated from a speaker beside my head. I jumped.

'Yeah – Saint Mary's.' I rubbed my eyes, imagining that there had been censure in the voice and wondering if I had made the right call after all.

'Why the cemetery – why not a church?' asked Ortega, tapping his fingers on his bent knee.

'If we take Norah to a church, there'll be a Priest in the firing line. In my experience, they tend to get in the way when they hear the word 'hell'.' I looked out of the window, remembering poor Father Harry. He really should have listened to me about his imp infestation. They hadn't been in church to listen to the gospel and they hadn't been vegetarians.

'Wouldn't that be a *good* thing?' Ortega flinched at the expression that settled over my face. 'I mean, couldn't we do with the help?' He looked me up and down, unimpressed.

I sneered at him. 'No,' I said flatly. 'This isn't an ordinary exorcism any longer. The beast is *connected* to Norah. We'll get her somewhere safe, where no one else can be hurt, then I'll find a way to deal with the problem permanently. A cemetery is the best place for her right now.'

Ortega leant forward, sceptical. 'What about mourners? What if there's a funeral going on?' He spoke as if I was too stupid to have considered those things. I briefly considered knocking him on the head with Matilda and had to fold my fingers to keep them away from her.

'A normal cemetery would be quiet this time of day,' I forced a shrug. 'Saint Mary's will be dead. There haven't been any burials there for four years.'

'Are you sure?' Ortega leant back again, his tone condescending. 'A cemetery in central London, there's no way it's closed.'

I looked out of the window. 'Trust me . . . it is.'

The car turned and I gripped Matilda's handle, seeking comfort. I didn't believe in fate, but after Gran's insistence that she'd seen Danny, the appearance of the book and then a trip to the cemetery where he'd died, seemed odd coincidence. But, no, Norah needed hallowed ground and the cemetery was the nearest to my flat. I let my shoulders relax. There was no cosmic conspiracy.

'When the car stops, we need to run for the gate.' I turned my attention back to the interior of the car and kicked Norah's rucksack across to her. 'The hound has your scent now but put this on anyway, it might buy us some time. If it takes a while for it to figure out where you've gone, that's even better.'

Ortega leant across me, half pinning me to the seat. His spicy scent filled my nose and I turned my head away as he pressed the button. 'Give us a two-minute warning before we stop please, Andrews.'

'Sir.'

As Norah put on her rucksack, Ortega picked up the book.

'We could leave that here,' I said, suddenly not wanting it anywhere near me.

'Then how will you use it to work out how to fix things?' He asked, tapping the cover. 'Where I go, it goes.'

I scowled and Ortega blinked suddenly, his eyes going to my mouth. 'Don't do that.'

'What?'

'Make that face.' He sneered. 'You look like a rabbit that's been kicked.'

'Screw you,' I said, and looked out of the window just as the speaker fizzed.

Andrews' voice filled the back of the car. 'Two minutes.'

Ortega gripped his sister's forearm. 'You ready to run, kiddo?'

Norah pulled her long hair back into a twist under her bandage and nodded, but her hands were shaking, and her hair ended up lopsided. She looked at the door and fidgeted, as if desperate to be off.

'I can hear it again,' she said, without looking at me. 'But it couldn't have known we were coming here . . . could it?'

Ortega stiffened. 'That's not possible,' he looked at me, his eyes narrowed. 'Or is it?'

'It's consecrated ground.' I licked my lips. 'Even if the hound managed to get here ahead of us, and I don't know how it could have, it can't get past the gate.' The car stopped moving so smoothly I barely noticed, but Ortega grabbed the handle of his sister's door. 'Ready, Norah?'

She fumbled with her seatbelt.

'Go!' He yanked the handle, shoved open the door and pushed her from the car. Norah stumbled, but Ortega was already leaping out after her. He grabbed her elbow and dragged her forward. The gate was right in front of them. He hit it at a run, but it didn't open.

Then I saw the chains. Ortega rattled them furiously. The cemetery was on lockdown – I should have realised.

I fought my way across the seats, no longer caring that I was leaving smears of blood on the leather. I wrestled with my crutch and fell out, head-first. The crutch landed on top of me. I lurched to my feet. 'This way,' I said, gesturing wildly, and Ortega turned. I was already limping along the wall, my crutch swinging me like a pendulum and rubbing hard on my new calluses.

Ortega shoved Norah ahead of him and she sobbed as she ran after me, quickly catching up.

'Where are we going?' Ortega looked back, and I followed his gaze. Andrews had remained in the limo, and, as I watched, the back of it hit the pavement with a crunch. A deep indent appeared on the boot, glowing red with heat. It was in the shape of a giant paw.

The car shuddered and another appeared on the roof, almost caving it in. Andrews must have put the limo into reverse then because the car lurched backwards. I hoped he had taken the hound at least a few metres away from us.

'How many of them are there?' I gasped.

'I don't *know*,' Norah wailed. 'More than one.'

'Run faster!' My mind raced – it had been four years since I'd been here and things looked different. The ivy had grown – where *was* it.

I lunged at the wall and started hitting it with my crutch. Norah shuddered behind me, teeth chattering.

Clunk, clunk, clunk. I kept hitting ivy covered stone. 'Where are you?' I screamed.

I looked along the wall and started. Danny was standing a bus length away from me, his head tilted to one side. His hair was as messy as always, his hunch distinctive and his expression serious. 'Sorry, Gran,' I whispered.

I jolted into motion, running towards him; half desperate to touch those hands again – but I'd forgotten my injury. Ortega caught me as I fell. 'No!' I cried. I looked up, but Danny had gone.

I regained my feet and limped forward as fast as I could. 'Danny!'

Behind me, Norah screamed but all I could think was where had Danny gone? I reached the spot where he had vanished but there was nothing, just the lingering scent of Lynx aftershave. He'd thought it so cool.

I felt a tear on my cheek and dashed it away. Then I spun to face the wall. Here the ivy was thicker, a ragged curtain of bruised leaves browning in the harsh summer afternoon. I lifted Matilda and hit the wall. *Clunk ... clunk ... thud.* I paused. Tried again. *Thud.*

'It's *here*,' I yelled. 'Quick!' I raised Matilda and slashed my way through the thick green drape. Behind was a small wooden door, almost child sized. I kicked it open and boards disintegrated under my boot. It was dark on the other side. I grabbed Norah's rucksack and, balanced on my good leg, I tossed her through.

I felt the rush of something huge against my back and tensed, but there was no impact. The hounds had not yet fully manifested. I thought of the damaged limo, glad that the damned dog hadn't thought to jump on *me*.

'Nicky!' Norah was shrieking.

Ortega halted next to me. 'How did you know this was here?' He took my arm. His hand was big; his fingers wrapped all the way around.

I swallowed. He hadn't recognised me then. I had wondered. I'd been in all the papers, but I really do have quite an ordinary face.

I was surprised too that none of the governors had given him my history, but they'd probably had better things to do after I'd left. I imagine they'd immediately changed the subject towards additional donations Ortega Enterprises might be willing to make to the school.

'Misspent youth,' I replied, thinking for a moment about Violet, Elena and Danny. Then I shook free, ignoring his narrowed eyes, ducked under the lintel and followed Norah.

It was dark on the other side of the wall, not only because the sun was behind the wall, but because there was a crypt in front of the little door. There was just about room between the two walls for me to sidle out of Ortega's way. Dragging Norah, I crunched my way through decades of dead leaves and mulch. Cobwebs clung to my face and I used my crutch to push them aside so that we could edge out of the narrow passage. The stone was slimy with algae that left green stains on my clothes. I hadn't remembered the passage being so tight.

Behind us Ortega grunted, but said nothing.

We emerged into dappled sunlight. Shade chilled my arms and I looked up. A crater-faced angel spread blunt wings overhead and I cringed from the memories – this was how we'd entered the cemetery four years ago. Elena in front, then Danny, then me holding Danny's hand. This was how it had all started.

I gave Norah a gentle push and she sidestepped to let her brother pass. He grunted as he squeezed into the light. I looked back and hid a smile. His expensive grey trousers were spiky with dead leaves and his white shirt was streaked with green and brown.

There was a spider in his hair. He still held the book.

'Now what?' He started to brush himself down, gave it up as a bad job, sighed and straightened.

'Now we get Norah settled, then we work out where Emporium is.'

'Settled?' Norah started. 'How long am I going to have to stay here?'

I shrugged. 'Longer than you'd need to if you told us where Emporium was.'

Norah tightened her lips and I strode forward. The first time I'd come here we had turned left, heading towards Vi's grave. This time I faced resolutely right.

The cemetery was huge and silent. You'd have thought there would be government bodies all over the place, but the rift wasn't dangerous in itself – you could walk through it with no ill effects. All the measurements that could be taken had been recorded years ago. Now Vi's gravesite was like a crumbling cliff edge – it had been cordoned off, the cemetery closed and that was all folks.

'Look at that,' Norah stopped at the top of a hill: below us there were rows and rows of overgrown gravestones, like monoliths growing from the landscape. From where we stood, under an oak tree, we had a wonderful view of the London skyline. The Shard glittered like a sword in a shaft of sunlight, reflecting both the winding Thames and the bright sky.

'The dead get the best real estate,' said Ortega, putting a hand on Norah's shoulder. 'Do you want to wait for us here?' She nodded. 'I'll get Andrews to bring some camping equipment and food.'

Norah's mouth dropped open. 'Camping?'

I snorted. 'What did you think – that there was a hotel in the centre somewhere?'

'I—I didn't think.' Norah folded her arms. 'Are you sure this is—'

'Take it or leave it,' I snapped.

'Can I at least get a takeaway?' Norah threw herself on the grass, her legs in front of her.

Ortega nodded. 'I'll have Andrews bring it.'

'As long as you stay here, you should be all right.' I rubbed my eyes. 'It gives us time. The hound knows where you are, but it can't touch this ground.'

'She can't stay here for ever,' Ortega reminded me. 'She has school.'

'School?' Norah stared at him. 'You're thinking about the *school* I'm going to miss?'

Ortega folded his arms and looked thoughtful. 'I can get Andrews to pick up homework for you.'

'You aren't serious?' Norah thudded on to her back, sending dandelion seeds into the air around her.

'Deadly,' Ortega replied, glowering at her. The sun tangled in his hair and flowed over his broad shoulders. It was a shame he was such a prick. 'We have a lot to talk about, but not right now.' He looked at me. 'The card?'

Wordlessly, I handed it over. I hadn't been able to see anything on it but maybe he would.

The card was onyx-black, with embossed gold lettering.

'Maybe there isn't any more information,' I said as he examined it. 'Perhaps they only give cards to people who already know how to get there.'

'Why give a card at all, if you can't use it to contact them?' Ortega turned it over in his long fingers. He looked at his sister, who was deliberately facing away from us.

'Come on,' he sighed. We might as well head back towards Andrews while we think about this.' He dropped to one knee beside his sister. 'Don't leave this spot.' Norah looked up at him, her eyes were bleak. 'You're going to be OK. We'll fix this.'

Norah shook her head. 'Maybe you *shouldn't*.'

'Excuse me?' Ortega dropped the words like glass shattering in a sink. He gripped her shoulder. 'Why would you say that?'

'I *called the hounds*, Nicky. I was going to spill innocent blood, although,' she looked at me, 'Mark really isn't that much of an innocent – you should have seen what he tried to do to me on Halloween.'

Ortega stiffened and I snorted.

'I'm going to fix this,' I echoed her brother. 'I won't let anything bad happen.'

Norah's dark eyes widened. 'But why?' She whispered. 'I've done nothing to deserve your help.'

'True,' I replied. I looked past her, my eyes drawn to the other side of the cemetery which seemed steeped in gloom in spite of the spearing sunlight. I couldn't see the remains of Vi's burial place, or the recording equipment that surely surrounded it. Only grave after grave – lines of the sleeping dead, peaceful in their rest. But it *was* there: the evidence of one night of horrible violence that had torn the world apart. 'It's my job,' I lied.

10

ANDREWS LEFT WITH the limo, a shopping list and clear instructions. To Ortega's horror, we were now sitting in a greasy spoon – my crutch leaning against the table leg, the smell of bacon and charred toast in our noses and the growling tinnitus back in my ears. A radio chat show rumbled in the background. I listened for a minute: they were talking about the BRP's demand for a general election, and some kind of proposed legislation – something about a registration. I tuned it out, leant back and enjoyed the sight of Ortega trying not to touch anything.

He used one finger to push the salt cellar nearer to me. It left a grease mark like a slug trail behind it and he covered it with a tissue-thin paper napkin. He was sitting with his heel on his knee again and his leg bounced.

'Well, Ortega, what d'you think?'

I smirked as two mugs of tea were put in front of us. Both cups were dyed brown with tannin. Ortega's had an old lipstick mark pressed to one side. A metal pot followed, with suspiciously yellow milk inside.

"Sugar?" The aging waitress offered me a basket. There were three types of sugar in paper packages. I shook my head. "We don't leave 'em on the table anymore," she explained. "The sodding kids eat 'em."

"Fair enough." I nodded sagely as she waddled back to the kitchen, scratching at her thinning bun.

'How is this place still open?' Ortega sniffed his tea, then placed it next to the salt.

'The builders love it,' I replied, gesturing at the site across the road. We were the only customers, but come lunchtime it would be standing room only.

Ortega looked incredulous and then raised the card again, his frown reappearing. 'Maybe it's invisible ink,' he said, flicking the card as if the movement would make something magically appear.

'Worth a try,' I plucked it from his fingers and pulled my lighter from my flak vest.

'What are you doing?' He reached for my hand, but I held the card out of his reach.

'You never wrote messages in lemon juice?' I shrugged. 'You need heat to read them.'

'I hardly think the business card is written in *lemon juice*,' Ortega said, witheringly, but he leant forward in his seat, tension in every line of him.

I put the card on the table and held the lighter close. The small flame burned hot and the card started to curl. No writing appeared.

I flicked the lighter shut and tucked it back in my vest. 'It could need magic words for all we know.'

Ortega nodded. 'Well, we've tried heat – what about cold? We could ask Typhoid Mary over there to put it in the fridge.'

I shook my head. 'I just don't think that's it.'

'It's not an anagram.' Ortega showed me his phone. He had pulled a list of words that could be made from 'Emporium'. 'Loads here, but none that make sense.'

'Opium,' I read. 'Immure, Rome, Peru.' I sighed. 'No, nothing logical.' I rubbed my eyes. 'I think its most likely a revelation spell. If Emporium is targeting people with an affinity to magic, using the spell correctly to uncover the address could be a kind of first test.'

'They're after teenagers,' Ortega said grimly.

I nodded.

'Do *you* know the spell?' Ortega asked.

I shrugged. 'There are *dozens* of revelation spells, if not hundreds, and it'll be tuned to *one*, also,' I pointed to myself, 'I'm too old now – I'll be twenty in a few months. The only magics *I* can perform are spell reversals and exorcisms and they're not strong magic. The Catholic church has been doing exorcisms for centuries.' I tilted my head at him. 'How old are you anyway? Did you ever spellcast?'

He shook his head. 'I'm twenty-two. I was eighteen when the change happened. Like you said, pretty much too old. I tried a couple of things – we all did – but nothing worked well enough to bother with.'

'Twenty-two?' I stared. 'Aren't you some big shot in your company? I mean . . .' I gestured outside, to indicate the limo. It wasn't there, but he got the idea. 'Or is Andrews just the babysitter?'

'Funny.' He tapped his fingers harder on his heel. 'I guess you could say I was fast tracked. I started running the UK branch of Ortega Enterprises after Natalie died and Dad left. I'd been groomed for it since I could walk anyway.'

'Your dad left?'

Ortega looked at me, his eyes hard. 'He runs an international operation, so his work takes him all over the world . . .' He looked back at his heel and frowned at his fingers as though he'd just realised they were tapping a beat. 'He trusts me to run things here. There's no need for him to be in London.'

I swallowed. I wanted to point out that perhaps *Norah* needed him in London, but I, of all people, understood that there was no point in saying it. Sometimes parents couldn't cope, and they left. I touched my phone. Dad would likely be calling in the next couple of days. He'd pretend that Mum sent her love.

Ortega stared into my silence, then back at the card. 'So, we find a teenager and make *them* cast the spell.' Ortega looked around as if young people would spring from the floor like skeleton teeth.

I shook my head. 'I'm not putting another kid at risk.'

Ortega nodded, but I sensed reluctance and stiffened. 'Andrews has good local knowledge,' I said as he started to drum his fingers once more, on the table this time. 'He knew about Saint Mary's. Do you think it's worth asking if he knows anything about Emporium?'

Ortega sat up and spoke in an undertone into his phone. Listened. Spoke again.

'He's going to ask around and get back to me.' He looked at me – his eyes were measuring.

'We've got a bit of time then,' I said. 'Let's talk about my job.'

'Oh . . .' Ortega's foot started to bounce on his knee and his brown eyes turned wary, 'that.'

'Yes, *that.*' I put both forearms on the table. 'You were wrong, Ortega. Your sister was hurt, but she *had* done something terrible. I didn't deserve what you did to me.'

Ortega's eyes slid from mine. 'I . . . apologise.' He looked up at me, and I was struck by how 'Danny' his expression was – that ducking of the head. Was it something all boys learnt?

His Adam's apple bobbed. 'I was upset about my sister, especially after what happened to Natalie. Can you understand? The thought of losing *both* of them . . .'

I nodded as he looked at his hands. 'You know Dad is out of reach. Our mother died when Natalie was a baby – there was an accident. Now it's all on me – *I'm* meant to control Norah.' He laughed bitterly. 'How am I meant to *control* a hormonal teenage girl? I can't understand her; I can't talk to her. It's like living in a minefield, with bombs going off every time I step wrong. She used to be so *sweet.*'

Unbelievably I found myself suddenly sorry for him; a thaw that warmed my bones more than the boiling tea.

'She'll settle down,' I said, thinking of my own teenage years. At least she hadn't yet set off an apocalypse.

'If she gets a chance,' Ortega spoke with low intensity. 'The thing that's after her – it'll kill her? You're sure?'

I nodded, then touched my fingers to the back of his hand. 'We'll find a way to stop it.'

'It wants innocent blood?' Ortega said, quietly. 'There must be . . .'

I pulled my hand back as if he burned. 'You'd sacrifice another kid?'

'That's not what I meant. I meant . . . blood *donation* maybe, or an *animal*. A sacrificial lamb – it's called that for a reason, isn't it?'

I exhaled slowly. 'That'd better be what you meant.'

'Of course,' Ortega replied. 'I'd never—'

'I don't know what you'd *never,*' I snapped. 'I don't know you. I just know what you'd do for your sister. "Destroy my life," you said.' I pushed my chair back and picked up my crutch.

'Where are you going?' Ortega asked, half-rising – the panic on his face making him suddenly appear younger than twenty-two.

'The bathroom,' I said. 'Don't worry on my account.' I hobbled across the cafeand saw the waitress watching Ortega with a measuring stare.

She winked at me. '*He's* a keeper.'

I followed the direction of her gaze. He was sitting again, that leg twitching, fingers drumming, looking like a model with his designer stubble, and warm brown eyes. I sighed. 'He's an asshat.'

Once in the bathroom I peeled my tracksuit bottoms down, tore off my tattered bandage and looked critically at the oozing wound. I really *should* go to a hospital and get it re-stitched. I thought of Norah and what I owed her – if I hadn't opened the rift, none of this would be happening – and sighed. I pulled a wedge of thick green paper towels from the holder on the wall and wadded them up, then I rewrapped my bandage around them. It wouldn't stop the bleeding, but it might stop me bleeding *on to* anything else expensive.

I pulled my tracksuit bottoms back up and splashed water on my face. I really did look awful – my hair was a rat's nest and my brown eyes were bloodshot. I looked pale and sick. I breathed into my hand. Yep, booze-breath. I leant my forehead on the cold mirror and let my halitosis mist it up beneath me. My eyes fell on the sink below me – cracked porcelain and crusty fittings. The tiles under my feet were sticky. Not somewhere to stay and take stock. I exhaled again.

I straightened and tried to detangle my hair. Not that I cared what Ortega thought, but I did have *some* standards and I *was* out in public. I finger-combed the knotty mess until it hung smoothly and dragged it back again into a ponytail that would at least keep it off my face. I looked at my face. Possibly that was a mistake. I sighed again, took my flak vest off and removed my checked shirt. I put the vest back on without closing it and wrapped the shirt around my waist – there, another layer between my blood and the rest of the unsuspecting world. That left me in my vest and sleeveless *I'm dating my fridge* T-shirt. 'Awesome.' I whispered.

I forced my shoulders back. 'Suck it up, Ivy,' I snapped. 'There's a kid out there who needs you to sort this mess out. And a really irritating ass who will only get out of your life when you *sort this mess out.*' I nodded. 'Way to be motivational, let's go.'

I hobbled back into the cafe and found Ortega on the phone, frown lines between his eyes. I sat and watched him – the way his long fingers tapped eternally against any hard surface: the leg of the chair, his shoes, the phone. Was it nerves? Worry about Norah? Or was he always wound this tight? I suspected he was. I wondered what being groomed to run Ortega Enterprises had meant for his childhood. Had he even had one?

Unthinking, I took a sip of my tea, flinched, grimaced and pushed it to sit next to Ortega's full cup in the middle of the table.

On the radio they were discussing another attack: two kids dead, this time in Leeds. That was three in a week. Whatever was happening, was happening faster now and I couldn't help feeling that the other shoe was about to drop. I just wished I knew how hard it would hit and if there was anything I could do to stop it.

On the other hand, I couldn't be the only one worrying about this. People cleverer than I was had to be working the problem. I touched my phone again; I had a couple of numbers I could call. Once I'd sorted this thing out with Norah, I'd use them and just make sure. I rubbed my ears as the muffled growling grew more irritating, and turned my attention back to Ortega.

He finally put the phone down and looked at me. 'Andrews is coming to pick us up once he's dropped some things off at the cemetery.' He looked out of the window, towards Saint Mary's, then back at me. His dark eyes glimmered. 'You're dating your fridge, huh?'

'He's reliable and he feeds me,' I said shortly, clipping my vest closed. I stared at him – at his clothes, his haircut – this was a guy used to giving orders, not taking them. It could cause problems down the line. 'You know I'm the expert here, right?' I said, leaning forward. I was small, occasionally cute and never intimidating, but I used everything I had to stop him thinking that my stupid T-shirt was all there was to me. To make him believe that I'd had that security job for a good reason. 'When we find Emporium, if I tell you to do something you need to do it without question.'

'Wait a minute!' Ortega straightened.

'If I tell you to do something, it's probably because I've seen something you haven't,' I continued. 'I've been doing this longer than you think. I guess you could say I was fast-tracked too.

About *this*, I know more than you. I'm not a stupid kid. I've faced things you've never seen in a board room.'

'You've never been in one of my board rooms,' Ortega muttered.

I stabbed a finger on to the table in front of him. 'Do you want to save your sister?'

He glowered. 'You know I do.'

'Then you have to listen to me.' I released his eyes and sat back again. 'I'm going to help her, but if you get in my way . . .'

His mouth twitched; his natural arrogance at war with his love for his sister. 'I get it,' he said at last. 'She could die.'

'She *will* die, horribly.' I wasn't ready to let him off. 'And her soul will be torn apart.'

Ortega nodded. 'I get it.'

'Do you?' I sighed. 'I know what I look like. I'm not Black Widow. I'm not even Sarah Connor.' I shifted my gaze to the window. 'I'm not going to turn out to be a magical savant. I'm no Gin Blanco.'

'Who?' Ortega looked blank.

'Assassin, elemental magic. You don't read . . . never mind.' I shook my head. 'Just know that I will fight for Norah, because I have my own reasons to.'

Ortega's eyes clouded over. 'Are they good reasons?' he asked quietly.

I nodded. 'The best.'

The door opened and my eyes flicked upwards. Andrews loomed in the doorway, the wire from his earpiece twisting down his neck. The waitress dropped a cup with a squeak and my lip twitched. 'Besides, I don't need to be Wonder Woman with him around.'

'Why do you think I hired him,' Ortega said, standing. 'Ready?'

'Are you?' I tilted my head to one side. My ponytail slid annoyingly over one shoulder. I probably looked about sixteen. I suppressed a sigh.

He nodded.

11

ANDREWS LOOKED, IF possible, a little sheepish. 'I've got nothing, boss.'

'Nothing?' That frown line was back. 'Not a single contact – no one willing to roll for the right money? Not a *whisper?*'

Andrews shook his head and I'm sure I saw him toe the ground. Seriously?

'All right, don't worry.' I felt inexplicable pity for the giant chauffeur. 'I have one idea – it might not pan out but . . .' I rubbed my eyes. 'I *really* didn't want to do this.'

'What?' Ortega rounded on me. 'If you know something, you *have* to—'

'I *know*,' I growled. I opened the limo door and slid inside. 'I know a kid who seems like the Emporium type – she owes me a favour.'

* * *

The house looked pretty much as I expected it to. Full-on English suburbia: red brick driveway, red brick walls, net curtains, a lawn manicured to within an inch of its life and box bushes lining the path.

A nervous tic appeared on the back of Andrews' neck the moment we entered the estate.

I made him wait in the car.

I imagined a minor-key horror theme as I crunched along the gravel and rang on the doorbell. It played Vivaldi.

I crossed my fingers behind my back as a figure appeared, distorted by the frosted glass of the PVC door. 'Please,' I whispered, 'please, please, pl—'

The door opened. Damn.

'Miss *Mann* . . . M—Mister *Ortega*! What are you doing here?' Mrs Worth trilled. She patted her rigid helmet of hair and her eyes fixed on Ortega – as far as she was concerned, I had just blinked out of existence. 'To what do I owe this *honour*?'

Ortega stepped backwards, putting me in front of him. 'Miss Mann will explain,' he said.

* * *

'You want to speak to Olivia?' Mrs Worth said again. She was wringing her hands, looking from Matilda to my flak vest to the blood on my trousers. '*Olivia?*' She said, as if hoping I'd got her daughter's name wrong.

'Yes, *please*!' I touched her arm. There was sweat on her upper lip.

'Is it to do with . . . the school . . . last week?' The sweat beaded more thickly and Mrs Worth wiped it off, smearing a clump of face powder into the lines under her nose. She swallowed.

'We just want to talk to Olivia,' Ortega said, surprisingly gently. 'Just talk.'

'She . . . she's a difficult child.' Mrs Worth appealed to him. Her lilac jacket was beginning to darken under the armpits. 'Whatever she's done . . . she doesn't think things through. Her father and I—' she swallowed again. 'Perhaps we didn't spend enough time teaching her *consequences*.' She licked her lips and rubbed her face again.

'It's just a couple of questions,' I said. 'We don't think she's involved, we—'

'You're looking for a scapegoat, aren't you?' Mrs Worth cried suddenly. 'You're not going to let your sister get sent to the Commission for this, are you, Mr Ortega. Not an *Ortega*. So, you're looking for someone else to pin it on. Isn't that right? Well, it won't be my Olivia.' She retreated towards the stairs, the thick carpet absorbing the sound of her court shoes so the only sound was the dull thud of her feet and her panting breath. 'Olivia,' she shrieked. 'Run. *Run!*'

'For Christ's sake.' Ortega elbowed his way past her. 'We just want to *talk*.'

'Run, Olivia,' Mrs Worth leant weakly against the wall where Ortega had shoved her – one hand on her heart and the other on her hair. 'Don't tell me where you're going,' she shrilled. 'It isn't safe!'

I rolled my eyes and caught sight of the photos along the wall. They were all of a blonde little girl with corkscrew curls and a smile that failed to meet her cornflower blue eyes. When the hair started to darken to that dirty brown that blondes sometimes developed, the photos stopped. It was as though the little girl had died, but I recognised those eyes. I looked up.

Olivia Worth was standing at the top of the stairs. Her blonde hair was dyed now, and her arms were folded. 'What's going on?'

* * *

We sat in the limo. Olivia had insisted on a ride and who was I to turn her down. Plus, it was the best way of stopping her mother from eavesdropping.

'She thinks you're taking me away.' Olivia looked at her mother, who was ugly-crying at the end of the driveway. 'She thinks I'm never coming back,' she added, her tone thoughtful.

'She loves you very—' I started.

'Save it.' Olivia prodded the seats around her. 'Have you got a drink in here? Champagne?' Ortega handed her a coke. 'Huh,' Olivia snorted as she cracked the top and took a long drink. She'd stopped looking at her mother in the mirror and leant back. 'You want something?' She looked at me. 'I knew you'd collect.'

I shook my head. 'That's not how I operate, I never intended—'

'Whatever.' Olivia shook out her hair. 'What do you want?'

As I blustered in my attempt to prove that I wasn't the terrible person everyone seemed to think I was today, Ortega handed her the business card. 'You know it?'

Olivia turned it over in her fingers but didn't look down. Instead she stared out of the window at the passing houses.

I leant forward. 'We just need to know where it is.'

Olivia's mouth was a thin line as she met my gaze – her eyes were steely. 'Do you know what you're asking me?' She tilted her head. 'Do you know the oath I'll have to break to tell you?'

I glanced at Ortega and thought of the little girl in the photo that Norah carried. Neither of us had been willing to risk Natalie's soul to save Norah, yet for some reason it had seemed acceptable to put pressure on Olivia to make a similar sacrifice. 'Stop the car,' I snapped. As Andrews pulled into a layby, I slid out. 'We can't do this,' I said, leaning my head on my arms. 'I wasn't thinking.'

I expected Ortega to start yelling but when I opened my eyes, he was sitting opposite Olivia looking thoughtful and pale.

Olivia climbed from the car and stood on the grass. 'What're you offering?' she said eventually.

I stared at her. 'What?'

'I owe you, sure, but this is a lot bigger than you not reporting me to the Commission. So, Mr Ortega there – he's got pull *and* money, and its *him* you're doing this for, right?'

I didn't correct her.

'What is it that you want?' Ortega remained in the car, but now his legs and arms were folded. This had suddenly turned into a business negotiation. Not my area.

Olivia licked her lips, and for a moment the skinny high school girl looked a lot like her mother. 'I want a future,' she said at last. 'I could ask for money, but I know that runs out.' She looked for a moment in the direction of her home and I wondered what had taught her that lesson. 'I want *security*. I want Ortega Enterprises to pay my way through university and then I want a guaranteed job doing something that interests me – I don't know what that is yet though,' she added apologetically. 'But I want a starting salary comparable to the highest-level graduate starters, and it has to be a job for life – I can't be fired. If I leave of my own accord, I want excellent references.' She flushed and stepped to the limo, gripping the door. 'I'll work, Mr Ortega. I'm not asking for a free ride. I'm not . . . I'm not the best at well . . . anything, but I won't be a problem for you. I just want a *chance*.'

Ortega held out his hand. 'Done,' he said. Olivia hesitated, then took his hand and shook it.

'I still don't think—' I started.

Olivia pursed her lips. 'Do you know what they make us swear on? The soul of the family member we love or loved the most.' She laughed. 'They've got a way of making sure you're telling the truth. That you really have named the person you're closest to.' She smiled then, a wry twist of a thing that chilled me. 'I can't stand my parents,' she said. Then she sneered. 'The only family member I could ever bear at all, was Nan,' she laughed a little, 'and she was a right cow.' She pressed her lips together. 'So, you needn't worry. There's no sweet old lady being dragged off to hell – I'm pretty sure she's already there.' She flicked the card that she still held in one hand. 'I'll tell you where Emporium is.' She slid back inside the limo and leant her head back on the seat. 'I just hope Norah's grateful.'

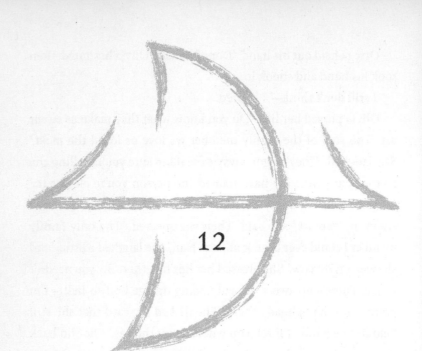

12

I STARED AT THE warehouse. Unbelievably, Olivia had given us directions to an alley right behind Saint Mary's cemetery. The high dusty windows above us looked out over the abandoned gravestones.

'This feels weird,' I said, shuffling my feet. 'It's too... convenient, or something, I don't know.'

Ortega folded his arms. The *Necronomicon* was in a bag slung over his shoulder. 'Norah's out there.' He stared past the building, as if he could spy her small campsite amongst the crypts. 'And she can't spend the rest of her life in a tent.'

'Something isn't right,' I ventured – my instincts were rarely wrong. I wish I'd listened to them four years ago . . . and I had a feeling I was going to wish I'd listened to them now.

'My sister needs us,' Ortega replied. 'So, whatever this shop is like, I'm going in.' And he marched towards the door.

I grabbed his arm and his muscles bunched under my touch. I teetered on my crutch. 'If they're after kids, they might not just let you pass. There could be protection spells.'

He stopped. 'You think so?'

'I don't know.' I bit my lip. 'They must have staff, but they could have amulets, or . . .'

'You're saying we might not get past security.' Ortega looked skeptical. I saw his point; the building looked like nothing. It certainly didn't match the glossy business card he was turning over and over in his fingers.

I'd been hoping we'd see someone else, another customer or client – someone we could follow in or at least copy. But the alley remained eerily empty.

'I don't like this,' I said again, as a dusty copy of the *Metro* blew past my ankles and tangled on my crutch. I shook it off. From the street at the other side of the bins, there was a burst of noise and light as a door opened and then closed, the shush of a bus pulling into a stop, the rumble of a distant train, traffic beeping, shouting, a smattering of laughter.

The alley seemed to absorb all sound; it was a sink hole at the edge of the city.

'Why haven't I heard of this place?' I turned my attention to the narrow wooden door. It didn't seem large enough for the building in front of me. 'If something's a threat to kids, I should've known about it. It's what I *do* . . .'

Ortega shrugged. He didn't seem impressed by me, so I guess he wouldn't be surprised that I'd failed to do my job. And that's how I saw this omission . . . a failure.

'I want my job back,' I repeated. 'Before we go in, I want an assurance . . .'

Ortega nodded. 'It's only fair. I'll speak to the Board of Governors.' Then he looked at me. 'Is that all you want?' He spread his hands. 'You've got me over a barrel . . . you could ask for anything.'

'Anything?' I hesitated, my mind flickering over my options. 'A raise?' I rubbed my eyes. 'Gran wants a holiday, so I wouldn't mind if a bit of a bonus came my way – a 'sorry for firing you and thanks for stopping the kids getting eaten' thing, but, I mean, what else would I . . .?'

"Is that all?" He looked surprised and I folded my arms.

'Let's get one thing clear. I'm working this problem so that I can help your sister. She's an idiot, and I wouldn't be averse to letting the police and the Commission know about her murder attempt but, the fact is, she's a teenager and it's my job to protect her.'

I loosened the strap on Matilda, marched past Ortega (definitely one of my top three dramatic moments – very satisfying) and I put my hand on the wooden door. It wasn't so much that I enjoyed taking charge but, as you may have already noticed, basic spells don't affect me much. I always figured it was because I was there when the rift opened and was exposed to the first dark matter that broke through. If there was a protection or distraction hex on the entrance, I could probably ignore it.

The wood felt . . . like wood. I took a deep breath and pushed. The door didn't open. I hadn't really expected it to. There was a lock about where you'd expect one to be. I pulled Matilda out of her sheath.

Wood splintered under the machete and, once I'd hacked the lock out, I balanced on my crutch, raised a boot and kicked the door in.

Part of me wanted to grin smugly back at Ortega, who'd been watching with a studiedly blank expression – but if something was going to burst out at us, I wanted to be ready and so I kept my eyes on the doorway.

For a moment nothing happened; there was only darkness behind the door. Then lights flickered on, one after the other, illuminating a long corridor. I watched it for a good minute, just in case someone – or something – materialised, but it remained a bare concrete tunnel.

Ortega touched my shoulder. 'Do we go in?' he asked. His touch was light, but his fingers were warm – almost hot – and I could feel them through my T-shirt. I shook him off.

'It's a kill box,' I said glumly.

'A what?'

'A kill box. If something comes after us in there, there's no room to manoeuvre, nowhere to hide, nothing to use as a weapon and only one direction to run . . . a kill box.'

'So . . . we're *not* going in?'

'Just follow me.' I stepped over the threshold.

My boots rang on stone and the bung on my crutch sucked at the smooth surface, tocking along rhythmically. Behind me, Ortega's leather soles slapped expensively. To his credit, there was no hesitation in his step – he was right with me, his breath, loud in the enclosed space, even and careful. For a businessman, he was holding up pretty well. If I'd have been a betting girl, I'd have laid money that I'd be on my own by now, or that he'd have sent someone else to keep an eye on me while he went back to work. But he was still here, standing up for his sister. It was weirdly comforting to have him there. I smirked to myself, he was also bigger than me; if a monster burst into the tunnel, they'd probably want to eat him first.

'I don't need to outrun the bear,' I muttered.

'What?' Ortega caught me up in two quick steps.

'Nothing, just an old joke.' I licked my lips. 'I don't need to outrun the bear – I only need to outrun *you*.'

'You're on a crutch,' Ortega pointed out acidly. 'You're not outrunning anyone.'

I sighed.

Apart from the fluorescent strip lights, there really was nothing in the corridor, not even dust. At the end, there was a stronger door – thick metal, with a scanner that looked a bit like a credit card reader set in the wall to one side.

I hefted Matilda. If I hacked at the scanner, exposed enough wires . . .

Ortega's arm appeared over my shoulder. He slapped the Emporium card on to the screen.

There was a moment of silence before the lights glowed green, making it feel as if we'd just been dunked underwater, and the door slid upwards.

I looked around. 'OK then.'

Ortega returned the card to his bag and looked smug.

I turned back to the new doorway. This time it was not an empty corridor that greeted us.

'It's still the middle of the day, right?' I said, blinking. Surprise made me retreat into Ortega. He didn't move, instead his hands encircled my upper arms, holding me in place.

We stood on a mezzanine. In front of us a darkened space, larger than the school hall, was lit by glowing night sticks and flashing bulbs. They cast green and purple light across the walls in a mesmerising aurora. One level below us, the floor was filled with writhing teenagers. They danced with wild abandon – naked limbs on display, open shirts and closed eyes. Hands tangled in hair and swaying arms rose out of the mass like branches of a forest. A dread-locked DJ hunched in a booth, his eyes glittering as he whipped up his worshippers.

I touched my ears, thinking my hearing had blown, but the rumbling growl continued to form an eerie background track which was driving me steadily crazier.

Ortega spoke in my ear, 'It's a *silent* disco.' He pointed, and I saw the headphones. 'Do you think Norah . . .?' His voice was loaded with disappointment.

'No.' I shook my head. 'She didn't come here to dance . . . and neither did we.' I looked harder. 'There has to be something more to this place – it's not *just* a rave.'

'There,' said Ortega, pointing. There were doors behind the DJ's booth – two were obviously toilets, but another was being watched by a man who made Andrews look as if he shopped in the petite section.

I nodded. 'Let's go.'

I sheathed Matilda and headed down the steps. With my torn tracksuit bottoms and muddy crutch, there was no way to blend in. Luckily the teens paid me no attention unless I jostled them and then it was a quick glance, a jeer and dismissal. That's one advantage to looking the way I do (at this point like Nancy Drew after a traffic accident) – invisibility to the terminally trendy.

'Are you the dealers?' A breathy girl latched on to Ortega's arm, flicking bright purple hair from side-to-side in a way that might be alluring in a few years, but still looked like she was a kid practising in her mum's mirror. She wore thick wedges that made her teeter off-balance on impossibly skinny legs, like a baby giraffe. A tight blue dress hugged her non-existent curves. 'My friend says you must be.' She pointed behind her and Ortega stiffened.

'Why aren't you in school?' he snapped.

'What's the point of that?' She laughed. 'Come on, hook us up!'

'What makes you think I'm a drug dealer?' Ortega said in a voice that made me shiver.

The girl was oblivious. 'It's obvious isn't it?' She frowned. 'You're well old.'

Ortega glared down at her long enough that she blinked up at him, released his arm and staggered back to her friend, frowning prettily and shaking her head.

I fought a smile. '*Well* old.'

'She was younger than Norah,' Ortega said, and scrubbed his hands through his hair looking confused and miserable.

I nodded. 'I can protect them from a lot, but from themselves...?' I shook my head.

Ortega put a hand on my back. 'Let's get this over with.'

My crutch helped me clear us a path through the mass of sweating bodies. It was creepy, not being able to hear the music. There was only the thump of feet, the slap of skin-on-skin, laughter, grunts, moans and a faint rhythm, tinny from the headphones that surrounded us. Yet the teens moved in concert to the inaudible beat – swaying into us, pressing against each other, their pupils huge in the darkness.

We wound our way slowly across the dance floor, Ortega glaring left and right so icily that anyone trying a stealthy approach quickly headed off.

'I was wrong,' I said as we reached the DJ booth.

'What?' He looked down at me.

'*You're* the bear.' I held up a hand to halt his forward momentum. 'What do we do about *him*?'

The man watching the door stood like he was carved out of teak, only the rise and fall of his chest betraying his animation.

'Let's try using the card again.' Ortega stalked forward, holding the Emporium card up like a ticket. He stopped in front of the bouncer.

The man looked down, his chin moving so slowly he hardly seemed to be turning his head. Then his eyes flickered past the card towards Ortega. He curled a lip. 'I don't think so.'

I sighed. 'It was worth a try,' I said, as I unhooked Matilda from my belt. While the man's attention was on the giant knife, I kneed him in the nuts. Never let it be said that I won't use every weapon at my disposal. The bouncer collapsed like wet cardboard, his face a mask of disbelief. I stepped over him. The door behind him wasn't locked and we stepped through.

'I thought Devon would keep you occupied a *bit* longer than that.' The voice was familiar, speaking in an accent that reached back into my throat, grabbed my guts and twisted . . . hard.

I reached blindly backwards, hardly realising I had caught Ortega's hand. It *couldn't* be. There had to be lots of people who sounded like *her*. My mind had only jumped to Elena because I'd seen Danny – I was primed.

'This is a *shop*?' Ortega said, his fingers gripping mine.

'Actually, it's a magic *Emporium*,' the voice replied, as its owner stepped into the light. '*My* magic emporium.'

She was almost exactly as I remembered her. She'd cut her hair so that the white blonde framed her face in a ragged spiky cut. She'd grown a little taller, a little thinner, a little bustier. Only her eyes had really changed – she was my age, but she had the eyes of a much older woman – cynical, cold and calculating. She was wearing a lot of wine-coloured leather, which somehow managed to leave a great deal of bare skin on display.

'Elena.' I tried not to sound as shocked as I felt. 'It's been a long time . . . you look good.'

She looked me over with a cool assessment that made me feel as if I was a new item of stock she was considering shelving. 'You look like hell.' She glanced at our locked hands. 'New boyfriend?'

I thought instantly of the young Danny and released Ortega. How could I feel as if I was betraying a dead boy?

'You two know each other then?' Ortega strode forward, eyes flashing, and I took the chance to peer around the 'Emporium'. It reminded me of an extremely upmarket clothes shop; the kind I'd never enter. Only a few items on display, carefully recessed lighting, dark wood shelves.

But the items for sale weren't scarves and bags. I caught my breath as I recognised jars of rare herbs, steel needles, blank-faced dolls, a display of pentagrams and other jewellery, probably enchanted, and a shelf of razor-sharp knives with jewelled handles. Then there was a walk-in fridge with glass doors, like a high-end wine cellar. Inside I glimpsed bottles of blood, things floating in jars, animal skins.

It was my worst nightmare.

'The amount of damage this stuff could do!' I snapped my head back to Elena. 'You're selling this to *kids*?' If I'd found out she was dealing heroine to toddlers I couldn't have been more horrified. 'You, of all people! *You've* seen what can happen.' Behind the counter there was a bookshelf . . . and on it . . . 'Half a dozen copies of the *Necronomicon*! What are you thinking?' I held Matilda in a death-grip, my arm shaking with the need to destroy *everything*. 'God, Elena, a few kids with some of this could—'

Elena waved a hand. 'A few *rich* kids—'

'What?' She'd derailed me.

'Have you *seen* my prices?' She strode in a loose-legged gait to the counter and pulled one of the books. She opened the cover and pushed it towards me. I couldn't help myself; I peered down at the handwritten price tag.

'Five grand!' I blinked. 'A bit more than you paid for your copy.'

She shrugged. 'So, you see, I don't sell to just *anyone*. In this world, Ivy, the rich are going to screw the poor – does it really matter if they do it with a share index or a copy of the *Necronomicon*?'

As I gaped, momentarily speechless, she moved to close the book and Ortega grabbed her wrist. 'You sold one of these to my *sister*,' he hissed.

'Sorry, we have a strict no-returns policy.' Elena offered a wide smile.

'I don't want to *return* it,' Ortega hissed, still holding onto her, his long body covering the counter as if there was nothing between the two of them. 'My sister cast a spell and now there's a hell hound *hunting* her.'

Elena's lips curled. 'That seems unlikely. Who told you so? *Her?*' She sneered at me. 'There are no spells in there that turn on the caster like that.' Her wrist was reddening under Ortega's grip.

'There are if they get interrupted,' I said, slapping Matilda on the book. 'All spells snap back on the caster if they don't achieve completion. And what about the three-fold law?'

Elena waved a hand. 'Only true if you're a Wiccan and you believe that rubbish. What's your sister's name?'

'Norah,' Ortega said through gritted teeth. 'Norah Ortega.'

Elena's lips curled upwards. 'I remember her. Cute kid. She's not a Wiccan.'

'Certainly not!' Ortega released Elena's hand.

'So, you're telling me her spell didn't achieve completion?'

I stared at her. 'She called *hell hounds*. At a *school*. Kids were going to die. I exorcised one and used the *Necronomicon* to send the other back.'

'And that's the one that's after her?'

I nodded.

Elena rubbed her wrist and whistled. 'She called hell *hounds* ... plural? She's powerful.'

Ortega slapped the countertop. 'Not the point,' he growled.

'No,' Elena pointed at me. 'The point is, your sister would be fine now if Miss *goody-goody* hadn't got involved.' She leant forward again, all pretence gone. 'Ivy Mann, who thinks she's so *freaking* perfect, well guess what – she makes decisions and people *die*.'

I gasped. 'Are you talking about Violet? She was already—'

'You don't *know*.' Elena snarled. 'You didn't give her a *chance*. Once she'd got out of that circle, she might have been *fine*.'

'She'd already killed Danny,' I yelled. 'You wanted me to give her *time*? You nut-job! Is that why you left me to deal with everything – with the police and the government and *everything*? Because you thought I should have let her *out*? To kill us?'

'Get out.' Elena pressed a button under the counter. Her face was colourless, as if she'd died too that night and not quite come fully back to life. 'Get the hell out.'

Ortega shook his head. 'You have to stop what's happening to my sister.'

Elena looked at the doorway as Devon limped inside. 'You all right, Miss Monroe?' He glared at me.

'These people are leaving.' She gestured towards us, but Ortega grabbed the spell book and threw it against a display case. There was clatter as occult jewellery scattered on the floor. The book bounced and landed face down, its spine bent.

'Hey, there's no need!' Devon caught him by the wrist.

'You owe me for that,' Elena said, narrowing her eyes.

'What do I do to save my sister?' he yelled.

Devon shook his arm. 'Thought you looked like a gentleman.'

Elena looked at Ortega. 'Hell hounds crave innocent blood.' She turned her gaze to me. 'Let Norah complete the spell and feed the hound. Then it'll leave her alone.'

'And if we can't do that?' Ortega growled, shifting in Devon's grip.

'Can't?'

'Won't!' I snapped.

Elena shrugged. 'Up to you then. If she doesn't complete the spell, it'll come for her. I'm surprised she's still alive, to be honest.'

'She's on hallowed ground,' Ortega looked tortured. 'What if she just . . . stays where she is?'

I thought for a split-second that Elena looked sorry. 'It won't matter. If the spell wasn't completed, it'll still be feeding from her. That's how the hounds trace their way back. If it's feeding from her, then her life force will be draining by the minute. The stronger the spell, the faster the drain. She dies either way.'

Devon put his free hand on Ortega's shoulder. 'Time to leave now, Sir.'

'I'm shutting this place down,' I said, quietly.

Elena laughed. 'And how will you do that? I'm twenty. You think I don't have a backer? You have no clue how the world works, Ivy. You didn't then, and you don't now. Go back to Wonderland, Alice – the real world doesn't need your fairytale nonsense.'

I followed Ortega and the bouncer towards the door, looking back at Elena sadly. 'Maybe the world needs fairytale nonsense more than ever . . . did you think of that?'

13

'YOU HEARD WHAT she said. We have to get back to Norah!'
Ortega didn't look at me as he started back towards the
cemetery at a run.

With nowhere else to go, I limped after him – watching his
silhouette vanish into the deepening gloom of a London evening.
As I pushed myself faster, my mind raced. Was there really nothing
I could do to help Norah? Was I racing after her brother just so that
I could sit by him and watch her die? I stopped moving. Ortega
would never just sit and watch his sister die. He'd argue that she
had to complete the spell.

I groaned and touched Matilda. Nicholas Ortega and I were no
longer on the same side.

The thought was more upsetting than I expected it to be.

I leant against the cemetery wall and ivy tickled my neck. They'd have to come back this way – the spell wouldn't be any use in an empty cemetery, they'd have to go to a school, a park, a shopping centre. Anywhere there were a lot of kids. I groaned again. 'I hate my job.'

I hefted Matilda. It was no good staying here – if I waited at the hidden door maybe I could catch them by surprise as they left.

I let the crutch take my weight, leaning fully on the plastic handle as if my body had turned to wet cement. I was tired, I needed more pain killers, my ears were *still* ringing, and I couldn't face a hell hound in this condition. That meant the only way to stop more kids dying was to prevent Norah from recasting the spell. And *that* meant dealing with her brother. Basically, I had to put Ortega out of commission and stop Norah from leaving the cemetery.

Then I had to sit with her while she died. It was the only thing I could do.

I received several sympathetic looks as I clumped my way along the cemetery wall. I must look dreadful. That's what Elena had said anyway. I ignored the commuters and let my thoughts turn.

So, Elena was back. and she blamed me for putting Violet's revenant down. Blamed *me*! Fury made my grip hurt. I wiped suddenly sweaty hands on my trousers. 'I watched my boyfriend die,' I muttered. 'I had to set my best friend's corpse on fire, and *she* blames *me.*' A young man in a suit that was too big for him looked at me with wide eyes and crossed quickly to the other side of the road. 'Huh. She was the one who made us do the spell. It was *her fault,* all of it.' I straightened. For *years* I'd taken the blame for this messed up world. For *years* I'd been trying to atone. 'And it was her fault,' I yelled. 'Not mine.' I clenched my fist around Matilda. 'Breakthrough!' I whispered. 'But I've still got to stop the Ortegas.'

I had reached the door. I pushed dangling vines aside and leant in. The little passageway was dark and still. I could wait just inside, and Ortega wouldn't know I was there until it was too late. I could take him by surprise, and he'd have no room to manoeuvre. It would be my own kill box. I hated the idea. Still, I started through the door with my elbow and crutch brushing against the side of the crypt. Then I stopped: my elbow was wet. 'Gross, what the ...?' I looked down and froze.

My lower arm was smeared with crimson gore. I swallowed. 'Is that ...?' It was too dark in the tunnel to see. I flicked my lighter open and the guttering orange flame showed a sigil scrawled on the side of the crypt in what was clearly blood. It glistened, still wet.

I frowned. Ortega couldn't have done this. It hadn't been there earlier, and I'd been with him all afternoon. For some reason someone had been into the cemetery after we'd left Norah and had daubed blood ...

'*Ortega!*' I screamed and hurled myself forward, bursting out of the crypt tunnel in time to see him racing towards me with his sister in his arms. Behind him, huge and horribly corporeal, raced two slavering hounds. Their claws dug divots out of undisturbed graves. Drool and mud flew, their eyes glowed and they snarled – a low terrifying rumble that reached into my gut and congealed the blood in my veins. They were as big as lions, but covered the ground like engines, their muscles gleaming as they moved like pistons. A third beast held back, watching more warily, prowling its way slowly through the gravestones.

The hound hunting Norah had learnt and brought friends. Great.

I didn't even think. I threw the crutch and limped towards the nearest pair, raising Matilda as I ran.

Ortega sprinted past me – Norah's weight hardly slowed him down. The beasts were only just behind him. I dropped to the ground, raised Matilda and swung her in a circle. There was a whine, a splash of blood and a thud. One of the hounds came down on a leg that was suddenly shorter. It collapsed, bowling over its snarling partner as it went.

I rolled back to my feet, bell at my belt tinkling like Christmas, and slashed the second hound across the eyes. Then I limped as fast as I could after Ortega before I could gauge the effect of my attack. It wouldn't slow the beasts for long, but I had their blood on Matilda now. If I could reach safety, I could exorcise them. I reached the crypt and glanced at the battered angel. I had caught its outstretched stone arm and was swinging myself upwards before I realised I'd even worked out a plan.

I dragged my bleeding leg behind me as I climbed, panting desperately, certain the hounds would be tearing me down any second. But although I was clearly the greater threat, they remained focused on their prey.

The passage was too narrow for them and one was blind, the other lame. It would take them a short while to work out they'd have to jump the wall. They snarled and growled, pawing at the ground by the crypt.

I sat on top of the grave, behind the stone angel, weeping with fear. My flak vest still contained my Bible and I fumbled in my belt for the bell and flare.

I had to put Matilda down. I didn't like it, but I only had two hands. I flicked the book open, lit the flare and rang the bell. As soon as the tinkling sound reached the hounds, they stopped growling at the wall and turned to face me as if their heads were on turntables. They stalked forward, looking bigger by the second.

I gasped and gripped the angel's arm with my thighs. '*In the name of God the All-powerful, Father, Son, and Holy Ghost, of the Blessed Peter, Prince of the Apostles, and of all the saints, in virtue of the power which has been given us of binding and loosing in Heaven and on Earth, I exclude you from the bosom of Earth, declare you anathematised and judge you condemned to eternal fire. I deliver you to Satan.*' I'd said the whole thing in a fast gabble. I hoped it would still work.

I rang the bell one last time, threw the flare at the lead hound as it started to leap for the crypt and slammed the Bible shut. The animals howled and vanished, one of them in mid-air.

I sagged on top of the weathered stone. 'Losers.'

I looked out at the third hound, which remained unbloodied and therefore unexorcised. It had stopped moving and its eyes glittered with a frightening intelligence. Carefully, it started to back away, fading into the shadows like a photograph left in the sun.

It would be back.

I picked up my gear, packed it away and looked over the wall. There was no sign of Ortega. I rested my head against the angel's. 'What have I done?' I climbed carefully down from the crypt and looked the statue in what remained of its eyes. 'I just saved the bad guys, didn't I? I never think. Where would they have gone?'

Unsurprisingly, there was no answer.

Ortega needed help, but he also needed lots of young people

and a place for Norah to recast the spell. The nearest school was the Catholic primary half a mile away. 'Please not Saint John's.' I shivered. There would be four-year-olds there, and I was sure it had a preschool attached. 'He *wouldn't*!' I wrapped my arms around my chest and shook my head. I was assuming a lot. I was imagining that I knew what this rich businessman would and wouldn't do, after knowing him for less than a day. And yet. 'Not babies.' I couldn't even consider it. 'Then, where?'

'Danny!' I whispered in quiet desperation. 'Danny, if you can hear me, I need a sign.'

I rotated on the spot, heart thumping as I looked for a teenage boy; blonde, unused to his height, hands like the paws of a puppy. 'Come on, Danny. Why are you here if not to help me stop this?'

There was nothing but the sighing of the wind in the trees. I sneered at myself, retrieved my crutch and edged back into the passageway. All right then, where would Ortega go? Somewhere nearby, somewhere he thought Norah would be safe, somewhere she could spellcast and that had lots of kids. I stepped on to the street.

Where would I go, if it were me?

There was only one place. '*Emporium!*' My crutch skidded on fallen leaves and I caught the wall for balance. 'It's perfect. There's equipment, there's security.' I thought of the teenagers dancing in eerie quiet, 'and there are victims.' I started walking again. A mother pushing a pram looked at me in quiet horror and sped up as she passed by. Perhaps I shouldn't talk about victims while smeared in blood and packing a huge knife. I limped as fast as I could back the way I'd come.

I *could* see Ortega weighing his sister's life against the lives of teens clubbing and taking drugs. But he shouldn't get to make that kind of decision. And, as far as I knew, none of *those* guys had tried to kill anybody – so there was that.

As I hitched my way frantically forwards, one thought kept intruding. Someone had daubed that sigil on that crypt. *Someone* had desecrated the graveyard – Saint Mary's was no longer hallowed ground. The only possible reason for doing it, was to let the hell hounds get to Norah. But no one knew she was there.

So, who could have done it? And why?

✳ ✳ ✳

As I approached the building, I realised that I had a major problem – no way to get in. Ortega had the Emporium card and, somehow, I didn't think Elena would be buzzing me past security. I stamped my way to the entrance and stood staring at the damaged door and the kill box behind it. If I went in, I might never come out. I was so tired. A traitorous voice inside me suggested that I could just let it all happen – let the Ortegas finish their ritual, then call the Commission to mop up the mess afterwards. I thought of the blank-eyed young girl in the blue dress and sighed.

'Come on, Ivy. Think!'

'Need a hand?' Olivia was standing in the alleyway, one hand on her hip, the other holding out an Emporium card. She tossed her blonde hair, a weary defiance in her eyes, as if she expected me to blow her off. As if she expected to be discounted.

'What are you doing here?' I stared.

'I came after you.' She shrugged. 'Figured you might need me. You don't exactly blend here, you know?'

'I know, but . . .' Her eyes slid from mine and her fingers tightened on the card. Her hand trembled. 'You *really* want to help?' I asked.

'You helped *me* out . . . before.'

'You don't owe me.' I hobbled nearer.

Olivia bit her lip and then looked up. 'No one likes me,' she said eventually, and her eyes flickered. 'You think I don't know that? I'm the mean blonde girl in the chick flick. I've got a 'clique'.' She made quotation marks in the air. 'None of them tried to stop me when I . . . you know.'

'Used that hex on Hannah Martin?'

'Yeah.' She swallowed. 'You could have hurt me, reported me to the Commission, instead you . . . talked to me. You listened.'

'No, *you* listened.' I leant against the wall with a sigh.

'You don't understand, I don't think anyone has ever taken the time to . . . forget it.' She straightened, and a hardness came into her eyes. 'Do you want in, or not?'

'I don't know what's going to happen in there,' I said, honestly. 'There could be hell hounds. I might not be able to protect you.'

'But you'll try.'

'Yes,' I nodded. 'I'll try.'

'Then let's go.' She marched into the kill box, heels clicking on concrete. She looked much more together than I did.

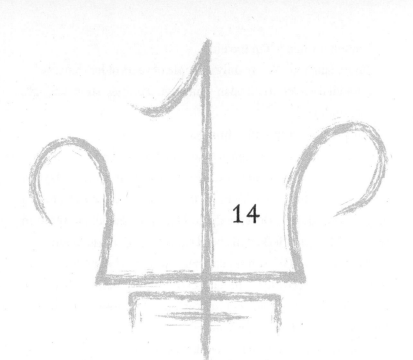

14

I HALF EXPECTED TO encounter running and screaming, blood and death; but the silent disco was continuing, the dancers oblivious to the danger they were in.

Olivia led me towards the Emporium, her blonde hair swishing behind her. I was surprised that I hadn't been stopped – someone should have been monitoring the entrance, but maybe the Ortegas had distracted them. We reached the door . . . and Devon, the bouncer.

He glared at me and covered his crotch. 'You again!' He opened his mouth to yell and Olivia quickly spoke.

'*Transibo et frigore.*' He froze. I looked at Olivia and she grinned at me 'It's a simple compulsion spell,' she jerked her chin. 'Even you could do it.'

I shook my head. 'I'm too old.'

Olivia laughed. 'You're only a couple of years older than me.'

I nodded. 'And you'll lose your own abilities soon enough, thank goodness.'

She pursed her lips and shrugged.

'Anyway, how did Ortega get past the human wall?' I looked at the frozen hunk. '*He* couldn't cast this spell.' I bit my lip. 'Maybe I was wrong – what if they went for the preschool after all?' I took a step backwards into the crowd and Danny appeared. He stood in front of Olivia and jerked his head silently towards the door.

'Who is *that*?' Olivia jumped, then she leant towards him. 'And *what* are you wearing?' She addressed him directly. 'That is so *out*.' Danny looked at me and then at Olivia. He frowned and then blinked out of existence once more.

'Danny!' I lunged forward, but he was gone.

'I think he wanted us to go that way,' Olivia murmured faintly, pointing to the door.

I put a hand on my chest. My lungs felt empty and I couldn't catch my breath. Danny had looked just the same as the day I'd lost him – he was even wearing the same goofy T-shirt and the bomber jacket his dad had brought him from America. He had ducked shyly when he looked at me. His eyes were the same, an urgent blue. A hand clenched my gut. God I'd missed him. But he couldn't possibly be here.

I nodded and stepped past the frozen Devon. The door opened at my touch. 'Stay behind me,' I said, and we walked into Emporium.

It looked much as it had the first time – someone had cleared up the mess I'd made but instead of the book on the floor, there was Norah. She was sitting propped up against the wall like a dropped puppet, her hands loose at her sides, her bandage loose on her forehead with black hair dangling in thick tangles over her pale face. Ortega stood by the counter, fists on the marble top, yelling at the camera trained on him from above. 'Get out here and *help her*!' His whole body was as tense as Matilda vibrating in bone. Dark hair curled over the back of his collar and his shoulders bunched furiously beneath his shirt. There was no sign of Elena, but *someone* must have let him in.

'Jesus,' Olivia whispered. 'Can I . . .?' She pointed at Norah.

I nodded. 'Be careful.'

Oliva crossed the room and knelt beside Norah. Then she transformed: her face went from concerned to ice-bitch in a second and she stood up. 'What *do* you look like, Ortega?' she said as she toed Norah's boot dismissively. 'Talk about low class.'

Norah's head lifted, she scooped her hair back and fire flashed in her eyes. "What are you doing here, Olivia?" She sneered weakly. "Are they letting just anyone in now?"

'Only the people who can get inside under their own steam.' Olivia tossed her hair. 'I see you had to be carried like an entitled little princess.'

Norah's eyes narrowed. Olivia stepped out of her reach and, after a moment, Norah fought her way to her feet. She reminded me of a calf standing for the first time. Olivia pointedly refused to offer her a hand.

Ortega heard his sister's moan of effort and spun around. 'What are you doing?' He caught sight of his sister standing beside Olivia, face flushed, and then he saw me.

'You're all right!' Relief relaxed his face. 'I didn't want to leave you to face those *things* alone.' His voice was earnest. 'But I had to think of Norah . . . you understand?'

'Of course.' I folded my arms over my crutch. 'What's the plan?'

'This place is protected, right? I figured she'd be safe here while we work out our next steps.'

'You want to see Elena?' I glanced at his fists on the countertop.

'*She* sold her the book,' he said stubbornly. 'This is her responsibility. If she doesn't fix this, I'll sue her so hard she'll be paying into the afterlife.' He shouted the last part at the camera.

'And that's the whole plan?' I tilted my head. 'You weren't intending to, say, use some of this magical equipment to get Norah to finish the ritual?'

His face hardened. 'What? No!'

'Not even if it's the only way to save her?'

'You don't think much of me,' he snapped, but his eyes slid from mine. I sighed.

'Elena, get out here and tell him.'

A door behind a cabinet slid open. 'I'm afraid Ivy's right, Mr Ortega,' Elena smiled as she glided forward. 'There's only one way to save your sister – I already told you that.'

'There has to be another. There're *always* options. If I've learnt anything in business, it's that there are always options.' He glanced at Norah. She was still on her feet, but she was swaying. Olivia watched her closely, saying nothing.

'In business, maybe.' Elena looked almost sympathetic. 'But not in magic. By the way,' she looked at Olivia. 'Is Devon still frozen?'

Olivia nodded. Elena sighed and waved her arm towards the door. '*Regelo*,' she called.

The reply was a moment in coming and muffled. 'Thanks, Miss Monroe.'

'How did you just . . .?' I frowned at Elena. 'You shouldn't be able to do that.'

Elena tilted her head, as though I'd said something crazy. 'Why not?'

'You're a year older than me.' I stepped closer. 'You're too old to perform magic.'

'Clearly, you're wrong.' Elena looked at me, really looked at me for the first time. For a moment I remembered long evenings in Danny's basement, the four of us hanging out, listening to Danny's music while Vi sketched and Elena posed for her. She looked so much the same. 'Are you telling me *you* can't?'

'Of course not.'

'I figured I kept the power because I opened the rift. But you did too, so if *you* can't . . .'

'She can,' Norah whispered.

I jerked and looked over my shoulder. 'No, I can't.'

'My sigils didn't work on you.' Her knees almost buckled, and this time Olivia did grab her, holding her steady but keeping her face carefully disinterested. 'You stopped the ritual – you banished that hound, remember?'

'I can do *exorcisms*,' I said, dismissively. 'Exorcisms aren't magic: the church has been doing them for generations.'

Norah shook her head. 'You must have read from the *Necronomicon* after you hit me.' She was gasping as she spoke: the effort exhausting her. 'To stop the hound. Didn't you?'

I started to shake my head, then stopped. 'Yes, but—'

'So, the magic words worked for you. They must have or . . .'

121

she tailed off. *Or there would have been a huge body count.*

I stared at her. 'We were lucky,' I choked out. 'You'd already started the spell, I just finished what you'd started.'

'It doesn't work that way,' Olivia supplied. 'You *can* do magic.'

'I *can't!*' I insisted. I tightened my grip on my crutch.

'Then you're stopping yourself.' Elena shrugged. 'You don't want to be able to spellcast, so you can't.'

I opened my mouth to argue, then hesitated. Was it possible that I *had* been blocking myself? The Commission had only stopped poking and prodding and trying to get me to re-run the rift spell once they thought I'd grown too old to perform. When I proved I could no longer cast a basic curse, but kept my weird immunity to spells, they mostly stopped bothering me and I got my job.

'Danny would have been—' Elena started.

'Don't say his name.' I leant closer. 'It was your fault, Elena. Everything that happened. You blamed me before, but *you* found the book, *you* wanted to do the spell, *you* raised Violet. Danny died because of *you.*'

With a sharp inhalation, Elena took a step backward.

'You blame me for what happened to Vi, but it was *you,*' I shouted. 'Then you *left* me.' I blinked back tears and my voice cracked. 'When Vi died I was there for you, both of us were, every day. We did whatever you wanted. We even raised the dead for you. But when Danny was killed . . .' I shuddered. 'When he was killed, you left me – to deal with the police and the *government,* to cope with his death, *on my own.*'

Elena froze. Her blue eyes had widened. The leather looked suddenly silly on her, like she was a kid who'd found a BDSM Halloween costume. 'You killed Violet.'

'A hit-and-run driver killed Violet.' I hobbled to the wall and leant against it. '*I* put down a revenant that would have eaten us both.' I shook my head. 'You can think whatever you want, Elena,' I whispered tiredly. 'But you had plenty of responsibility in what happened. If you can't face that, it's on you.'

'My parents moved us,' she said, avoiding my gaze. 'They wanted a fresh start . . .'

'Yeah?' I said. 'Well, you were lucky. Mine wanted a fresh start too. So, they left me behind.'

Ortega was staring from one of us to the other. 'If both of you can do magic,' he said, with false calm. 'Can you save my sister?' His fists were solid blocks on the counter, and he was trembling.

Wearily, I pushed off from the wall. 'I studied a translation of the book a couple of years ago. I don't remember seeing a ritual capable of breaking the connection between Norah and this hound. Am I wrong?'

Elena opened her mouth and a loud ding reverberated through the room. I jumped. Olivia looked briefly apologetic, but her eyes went to her phone. She gasped and held the handset out to Norah. There was a hesitation as Norah absorbed the contents of the screen, then she folded, and Olivia went down with her.

'What is it?' I limped closer, but Ortega beat me to it.

'Let me see that.' He took the phone from Olivia, who barely resisted. A teenager giving up her phone voluntarily – she must be devastated.

Ortega swore and showed me the screen. She'd received a message with a link – there were photos and captions. Someone had managed to make a joke of it, because there's always one, isn't there? It was something about hamburger. That's what it looked

like. No, not *it*. That's what the remains of the *kids* looked like –
raw hamburger.

I covered my mouth. Norah was already retching.

'That's what you stopped at our school,' Olivia murmured, as
Norah puked between her knees.

My chin dipped in acknowledgement. 'Where is this?'

'It's the all girls Grammar School in Kingston,' Olivia whispered.
'My cousin goes there . . . she messaged me . . .' She tailed off. 'She's
all right'

I pulled out my own ancient iPhone and looked for a news
site. Was this it – was this the climax the recent attacks had been
building to? It was my turn to lose my balance. I groped for Olivia's
free hand. 'Kingston's not the only one.'

Ortega scrolled through his own feed with trembling fingers.
'*Three* attacks. All in London. But . . . why?'

I looked at Norah, tears were drying on her cheeks. 'You weren't
the only one in London, were you?' I asked, trying to be gentle
although my voice shook. 'You were just the *first* one.'

Norah was shaking now, but Olivia pulled away from her. 'You
knew about this? And you didn't warn anyone?'

'I—I thought . . . after what happened with me, none of them
would go through with it. I called them and told them there was a
hound after me. I told them—'

'You *knew*.' Her brother's voice shuddered with disgust. 'We
could have saved those girls.'

Norah shook her head. 'I warned them – I didn't think they'd
. . . it's been almost two weeks.' Her breath was short and she
had to force her words. She barely had the energy to hold her
head up.

'All right.' I tried not to think about the pictures I had seen. 'That's enough.'

'They'll be raising their dead now,' Elena said, and there was a note of triumph in her voice. 'They'll bring them back whole, thanks to the sacrifice.'

'You knew about this too.' I stared at her. 'No . . . you *set this up*.'

Elena's shoulders went back. 'Everyone I sold the *Necronomican* to has lost someone, just like I lost Violet. They deserve a chance to bring them back.' Elena stepped quickly behind the counter, but not fast enough – Ortega was on her.

'How many dead?' He yelled. 'How many of these girls have families who will want *them* back? Will you give *them* the book too? People die.' He choked. 'Natalie died, and that's *horrible*,' he was speaking to Norah now, 'but it happened, and we have to grieve and let her go. It's natural.'

'Not this 'everything happens for a reason' stuff again!' Norah hissed from the floor.

Tears glimmered on Ortega's cheeks and my heart started to ache. 'You think I didn't love her as much as you did?'

Elena wriggled under his hold and I realised that his grip had intensified enough to hurt her.

'You think those girls didn't have brothers and sisters who loved them as much as you loved Natalie? What makes *us* so special that we get to defy death?' He dug his fingers harder into Elena's reddening arm. 'How dare *you* decide that some lives are worth more than others?'

'You do that every day!' Norah whispered. 'When you fire someone – how do you think they're paying for their heating, or food, or . . .'

'How can you think it's the same?' Ortega stared.

Andrews appeared in the doorway, an unfrozen Devon at his side.

'Andrews, is something wrong?' Nicholas flicked a hand. 'Why aren't you with the car?'

Andrews looked past Nicholas towards Norah. 'You hanging in there, Miss Ortega?' He asked.

Norah nodded. 'Yeah. Th—thanks, Andrews.'

'That's good.' Andrews raised a gun. Well, more of a hand cannon really. An American import for sure. 'And now we need you to complete your spell,' he said, as I gasped. 'It'll save your life and you'll be able to raise your sister. Win-win. That's what you want, isn't it?'

There was a lengthy, shocked silence. Then Elena sniggered. 'I wondered who they'd send.'

'What the hell?' Ortega dropped Elena's arm and stared at his driver. 'Andrews . . .?' He rubbed his forehead. 'I don't believe it. Why would you . . .?' He dropped his hands to his sides. 'When you say "we",' he growled, 'who exactly do you mean? Who are you working for?'

15

'YOU DON'T NEED to know that, Mr Ortega,' Andrews said, with none of his previous deference. 'All *you* need to know is that Norah will die if she doesn't recast that spell, and then you will have lost *two* sisters.'

'Norah isn't redoing the spell.' I pointed to the silent disco. There was no music to hear, but the stamp of teenagers' feet reverberated through the floor and made it feel as if I was standing on a train platform with an engine coming towards us. 'It'll be a massacre.'

'Ivy's right, she's not doing it,' Ortega snapped. 'And I want to know who the hell you are working for because it isn't Ortega Enterprises.'

'Don't you want to save your sisters?' Andrews stepped closer, away from a frowning Devon – his suit remained immaculate, but on one shirt sleeve I spotted a splash of crimson.

As Ortega stared, the answer stuck in his throat, I stepped swiftly under the gun, grabbed Andrews by the arm and pushed up his suit sleeve. The shirt underneath was blood-stained. He pulled back, but I clung on. I pushed the shirt cuff up to see unblemished skin. There was no cut.

'It was *you*.' I released him and he stepped back, shaking his sleeve back down. '*You* deconsecrated the cemetery. Whose blood is that?'

'Does it matter?' Andrews shrugged.

'Of course, it matters,' I yelled, as Ortega spoke over me.

'What does that mean – he deconsecrated the cemetery?'

'Blood on the crypt, that's what let the hound in after Norah.'

I started to lift Matilda and Andrews shook me off. 'I wouldn't do that, Miss Mann,' he said, firmly, turning the barrel in my direction.

Norah stared at him. 'But . . . Andrews . . . you've been driving me around for months. I thought we were friends?'

Andrews narrowed his eyes. 'With a kid like you?' He sighed. 'Look, Norah, cast the spell and then I can go back to my real job.'

'Which is?' Ortega said, through gritted teeth.

'Not babysitting you two.' He rolled his shoulders and cracked his thick neck. 'Don't make me force you.' He glanced at Devon, who cracked his knuckles like the caricature he seemed to be.

'Andrews let the hounds into the cemetery so you'd be forced to bring Norah here, where she'd have access to the equipment she needs for the spell. Isn't that right?' I stepped between the semi-smiling Andrews and the teen girls. 'You wanted to force the issue, but *why*? There've been attacks all over the country. Three big ones in London *today*. Why do you need Norah to spark *another* massacre?'

Andrews flicked his fingers, impatiently. 'Optimisation. The number-people worked out how many needed to die in order to force a regime change. Norah can help us topple the government. The kids that had the guts to follow through did well, but the Commission's people have already stepped in, exorcising the monsters they called and calming people down. It's a tinderbox out there, but we still need a spark.' He gestured towards the disco. 'An attack in a place like this, where the prey is boxed in and unable to escape – there'll be dozens dead, maybe hundreds. We're talking riots, civil unrest. The Commission won't be able to smooth it over. And when the people scream for change, *we'll* be ready to step in.'

'Oh my God,' I stared at him. 'You're working for the British Republican Party?'

'This is *politics*?' Olivia shrieked. 'You're letting kids die because you're trying to stage a *coup*?'

Andrews looked at her for the first time. Olivia was shaking, her face white but determined. She held her phone in one hand. 'Oh, please!' he laughed. 'You thought you could record my big confession.' He showed her his own device. 'Your phone's been toast since I walked in.'

Olivia looked at her phone, shook it as if that would revive it, and pressed her finger to the screen. She shook her head. 'It is,' she murmured. 'Sorry guys.'

'It was a good try,' Ortega said. 'Just to be clear, Andrews, there's no way we're going to murder hundreds of kids and, in case it isn't obvious, we've no interest in helping you fanatics take over the country.'

'Don't tell me you've become an altruist,' Andrews sneered. 'You forget, I've been driving you around. I know you.' He spread his hands. 'Look, you'll have your sister's back. Does the rest of it really matter?'

Ortega moved to my side and looked at me, almost warmly. I blinked my surprise. 'Yes, it actually does.'

'Oh, I see,' Andrews snorted. 'Well, Miss Mann isn't going to save the day here, Mr Ortega.'

I remained standing in front of the girls. 'You may as well leave, Andrews.'

Andrews shook his head. He sidestepped, not to reach Norah but so that he could meet her eyes. 'You're happy to let your brother speak for you?' he said to her. 'That isn't like you.'

Norah looked up at him through bleary eyes. 'I don't want to die,' she whispered.

Olivia tensed.

'But I already stopped the ritual and I'm not restarting it.' She shuddered. 'It was . . . horrible.'

Her brother shuddered and I tore my gaze from Andrews to see tears in his dark eyes – he wore an expression of pride. I smiled.

'We might be rich assholes,' he hissed. 'But we won't kill for someone else's messed-up political agenda.'

Andrews looked at Elena. 'Then can *you* cast the spell, Miss Monroe? My employers would pay extra.'

Elena sucked air between her teeth, like a dodgy mechanic offering to refit an engine. 'It's still linked to Norah's life energy, so technically . . .'

'Don't you *dare!*' I whirled on Elena, raising Matilda. I heard a click as Andrews cocked his gun.

'Don't move, Miss Mann.'

I froze. With one smooth step, Nicholas put himself between the gun and my body. Without another thought I tossed my crutch towards Elena and leapt after it. She batted the crutch away and found Matilda pressed against her jugular, my arm around her neck. Devon had lurched forward, but now he stopped and held still as I panted into her ear.

'If you even think about restarting that spell,' I growled, 'I'll bury Matilda in your throat. Don't think I won't.'

Elena held her breath, then she slowly raised a hand and Devon straightened.

Andrews sighed. 'Let her go, Miss Mann, or I'll shoot Mr Ortega.'

I shrugged. 'Shoot him.' I glared over Elena's shoulder – the peach scent of her hair product in my nose, the slick feel of her creaking leather on my bare skin. Nicholas's dark eyes met mine and he nodded carefully. I smiled. 'You hold no cards here,' I said. 'Norah isn't strong enough right now to do much about the spell, even if she *did* agree to do it, and Elena isn't going to be in any position to cast it for you ...' I squeezed her more tightly and Elena winced.

Andrews' fist tightened on his weapon. 'Then, Olivia—' he started.

'Fuck off.' Olivia didn't even look up.

'You don't know what I'm offering.'

She glanced at him. 'I don't need to.' Finally, she put an arm around Norah. 'If you knew anything about me, you'd know

I don't do well with authority.' She was shaking, but her eyes were hard.

Andrews' eyes slid from her as if she didn't even exist. He settled on me. 'Then what about you, Miss Mann? Do you want to be working in school security for ever? That's assuming the Ortegas actually do let you have your old job back.'

I flinched.

'Are you really happy with the way the country is being run? With the risks that kids take every day, just by going to school? You're a brave young woman, but there's only one of you. You can't protect everyone. The Commission is ineffective, it steps in *after* something has happened. What about the establishments you aren't standing in front of?'

I swallowed.

Andrews kept his gun trained on Nicholas, but he spoke to me. 'Join us and you could do something to protect *all* the kids. The Conservatives aren't doing enough to control magic. When the BRP is in charge, we'll put strong measures in place. We'll increase security in public areas, we'll have magic items safely removed and destroyed, regulate what appears on the Internet, make sure kids can't access spells or, if they can, that they can't get hold of the items they need to perform them. We'll have whole departments dedicated to stopping uncontrolled magic usage.' He took a breath and smiled. 'We'll identify and control the kids with the impulse to do magic and the power to make it happen.' He paused. 'We'll be able to use their talents for the good of the country.'

For a moment I let myself drift. Maybe he had a point. Regulation of magic didn't sound so bad. The lives that would be saved . . .

'There would be a role for you at the top of the department,' he started, with a slick smile. 'A flat in Mayfair, a company car . . .'

'And what happens to kids like me?' Olivia abandoned Norah, and stood. 'Miss Mann, you didn't tell the Commission on me before, but it sounds like this new lot would have me *identified* and *controlled*. Do you know what that means?' Her shoulders went back. '*I* do. Nan's family came over from Germany in 1938.'

I stared at Olivia. 'Oh . . .'

'Exactly.'

Andrews curled a lip at her. 'I should have shot *you* when I came in. In fact . . .' He stepped out of Nicholas's reach and turned the gun towards Olivia. 'You might not care about Mr Ortega, Miss Mann, which is a shame as he seems to feel something for you. But what about the smart-mouth here? Are you happy for me to shoot her?'

'You *wouldn't*,' Olivia sneered.

There was no change in Andrews' face – no smile, no narrowing of his eyes, no tension in the hand that held the gun. He simply squeezed the trigger.

I screamed and Nicholas jumped forward, but Andrews swung the weapon back towards him, stopping him in his tracks. Olivia hadn't cried out but she was gasping, as if her outgoing breath had encountered a blockage. She was clutching her stomach. Blood that looked too dark to be real, crept between her fingers. She swayed on her feet for a heartbeat and then Norah howled like one of the dogs hunting her, and Olivia collapsed as though her legs had disintegrated.

'Gut wound,' Andrews said, with a jerk of his gun. 'It'll take her a while to bleed out. Given the chance, you might be able to save her using that magic of yours.' He gestured with his free hand towards Norah. 'That's innocent blood spilling all over the floor – making certain assumptions of course – could be useful. Just saying.'

'Shut up!' Norah screamed. 'Just shut up!' She had removed her jacket and was holding it pressed against Olivia's wound, her own arms weak and shaking.

Andrews looked at me. 'I can shoot her in the head next,' he said, conversationally.

'Jeez.' Devon was staring at the blood spreading across the tiles like spilt oil – the edges breaking as the dark slick encountered grouted tile corners and spread into sharp angles – and the skid marks made by Norah's knees as she struggled to keep upright and compress the wound. His cheeks had hollowed, and he was holding his stomach as if he was the one who'd been shot. 'I didn't sign up for this. I'm meant to stand in front of the door, stop the ordinary kids going where they're not welcome. I get hazard pay for being frozen up so often.' He was gabbling, his big face crumpled and confused.

'What?' Andrews blinked. 'You're kidding me.'

'This ain't right.' Devon backed towards the door, shaking his head. 'Not at all. Ma's goin' to skin me alive!'

'Where are you going?' Andrews demanded.

'Shift's over. I'm going home. You ain't my boss, no matter what you said out there!' He tore his eyes from Olivia's tears and sped from the room, letting the door slam behind him.

'Can't get the help, huh?' I muttered, even as shock sent lightning-fast trembles through my limbs. I glanced at Nicholas. His gaze was fixed on Olivia, his mouth working as if he wanted to speak. He looked a little like a mannequin in a high-end store, frozen and plastic. Under my enclosing arm, Elena's breath was coming faster as if she was scared, or excited.

As Andrews opened his mouth to make another threat, Nicholas moved. He leapt clumsily into his former driver and pushed his arm towards the ceiling. The gun fired and I caught my breath, but a crack and puff of plaster showed me where the bullet had safely hit and I exhaled again. Nicholas threw a punch and managed to snap Andrews' bald head back, but Andrews snorted and I realised that against someone as well trained as Andrews had to be, a businessman, even one as fit as Nicholas, stood no chance.

Shoving Elena to one side, I limped as fast as I could towards the fight.

Nicholas was clinging on to Andrews' arm, preventing him from bringing the gun to bear and he was kicking frantically with his slick black shoes, but he was like a ten-year-old trying to beat up a decreasingly tolerant uncle. Andrews slammed a punch into the side of Nicholas's head and then I was there, skidding behind him and bringing Matilda's hilt down behind his ear. If this had been a film he would have dropped like a stone, but instead he spun around, using Nicholas's body like a ram, to slam into mine and send me flying into the wall. My injured leg took the brunt of the impact and I shrieked involuntarily as a shard of pain stapled me to the floor.

Andrews threw Nicholas to one side and his face contorted. 'Your interfering days are over, Miss Mann,' he growled. He turned towards me, his finger tightening on the trigger, and I could do nothing but press myself against the wall.

Then I blinked. Danny was standing in front of me, shaking his head.

Andrews hesitated. 'Where did you come fr—?'

'*Transibo et frigore.*' The quiet voice was wracked with pain and I looked up to see Olivia, holding Norah's hand. Both girls were looking at Andrew, their blood covered fists raised. Olivia was choking out the spell.

'Oh my God, Olivia,' I gasped. Andrews didn't move. He couldn't, the spell held him still. Carefully I slid out from under his reach and limped towards her. 'Stop! You don't have the energy. Neither of you do.'

'It's . . . done.' Olivia dropped her arm.

'Innocent blood,' Norah rasped. 'It'll strengthen the spell, hold him for a while.' She closed her eyes.

'Innocent-ish,' Olivia quipped. Then she started to cry. 'It hurts. It really hurts.'

'I know.' My hands clenched impotently around Matilda.

'I want to go home.'

'I know.' I should never have brought her inside. Failure was broken glass, grinding to powder in my gut.

Nicholas looked at Danny, who remained standing in front of Andrews, but said nothing. Instead he turned to scan the room, his eyes shifting as he sought the last person standing. To my surprise Elena hadn't fled through the rear door. She was standing with one hand on the handle, staring at Danny.

'You're here,' she rasped. 'I didn't think it had worked.'

'Elena, what have you done?' I used the wall to help me to my feet, glancing longingly at my crutch where it lay on the floor beside the counter. 'What did you do to Danny?'

Elena swallowed. 'It's not what you think.'

I stayed by the wall, but Danny turned to face me, and his expression was so wistful that I almost sobbed. He walked towards me, his feet sinking a little into the tiled floor as if it was an effort to maintain the appearance of normality. He raised a hand as if to touch my face and frowned.

'Yeah, I know,' I sighed. 'I'm older than you now.'

'Can he talk?' I hadn't seen Nicholas follow Danny over but now he stood just to one side of him, examining him as if he was a scientist looking down a microscope. Andrews' gun dangled from his fingers.

'Don't look at him like that!' I itched to take Danny into my arms, to hug him. He looked so lost. I glared past Nicholas, at Elena. 'I'll ask you one more time. *What* did you do? And how the hell did you end up working for the BRP?' I gestured at Andrews and saw a flicker of rage in those frozen eyes.

Elena's hand dropped from the door handle and she scraped her fingers through her hair, as if to pull the too-short strands out of her eyes.

Nicholas tore his gaze from Danny and half-raised Andrew's gun with a twitch of his lips. 'Answer her.'

Elena groaned. 'You don't need that. I am working with the BRP, or a branch of them, but not for the reasons you think.' She indicated the counter. 'Can I sit?'

I nodded and she hopped up on to the top, crossing her legs, consciously *Fatal Attraction*. Nicholas gestured with the gun. 'Hurry it up.'

Elena nodded. 'Our interests align. Temporarily, at least.' She put her hands on her knees, leaning forwards. 'The BRP want to use magic for themselves – to take over the country and then weaponise talented teenage spellcasters. Rift magic is restricted by distance from the rift itself and the sea surrounding us – go a few miles past the coastline and you can't do a thing, but you can perform magic on something *here* and take it over *there*.' She wafted her hand. 'Take your Gran for example—'

I frowned. 'How do you know about Gran?'

She ignored me. 'The spell that put her into the tabby is complete – there's no magic animating her. So, if you took her to France, the lack of rift magic there wouldn't kill her.'

I nodded my understanding.

'*I* believe they're picturing battalions of hounds, invisible spies, invincible marksmen, unstoppable plagues, that kind of thing. The BRP are picturing Rule Britannia, with the armies of hell behind us. And they won't be the only ones.' She looked at me intensely. 'Ivy, we have to close that rift.'

I stared. 'You want to . . . close the rift?'

'How does that align . . . with the world . . . domination . . . brigade?' Norah rasped.

Elena glanced at her and then back at me, her eyes as compelling as they had always been – driving Danny, Violet and me to do ever crazier things: duck out of class, go swimming in the canal, make fake online accounts . . . raise the dead.

'I haven't just been *selling* these books.' Elena nodded towards the shelves behind her. 'I've been researching, speaking to scientists, religious guides, everyone I could think of. I reckon I've got it worked out. To shut the rift . . . we have to *do the spell again*!'

She spread her hands, like she was saying 'ta-da'!

I stared. 'Seriously? You think that wasn't tried right off?' I rolled my eyes. 'You're hardly the first to do the research. How do you think Gran ended up the way she did?'

Elena hopped down from the counter. 'No, I mean *properly*. It has to be the same spell, spoken by the same people, in the same place, at the same time . . .'

'Danny's *dead*, Elena, in case you hadn't noticed.' I looked at him in quick apology.

'Why do you think I needed Norah and all the others?' Elena sighed. 'I was looking for someone who *can* successfully resurrect the dead – someone *really* powerful. We *need* to bring Danny back to life and have him say the spell with us. It's the only way to close the rift, the only way to stop *all* of this.'

'Oh God, Elena.' I put my head in my hands as she kept speaking.

'I found a bunch of kids I believed powerful enough to do it. Norah was strongest of all. Look how long she's survived with her life force being drained by *hell*. She *has* to recast the spell, Ivy. Then, if she can bring her sister back, she can reanimate Danny and we can end it *all*.'

I raised my head. 'And Danny's back, like *this,* because . . .?'

'You don't think I'd have jumped straight to a killing spree, do you?' Elena sighed. 'I tried to bring Danny back myself. I thought I was strong enough. This was the result.'

I exhaled. 'At least he isn't in the body of a cat.'

'Exactly.'

I closed my eyes, tiredly. 'You're telling me that the only way to close the rift is for Norah to redo the spell, raise her sister *and* Danny, then we have to wait for the 31st before we . . .' I tailed off. 'It's the 31st today.'

Elena nodded.

'You had this all planned out.'

'The timing. Yes, of course.'

'If Norah does this, more kids are going to die.'

'If she doesn't, the rift stays open. Who knows how many more will die because of it?'

I looked at Nicholas. His handsome face was pale. 'What do I do?' I asked him.

16

I WATCHED NICHOLAS THINK – his fingers drummed on the counter as his mind raced. Then Olivia groaned, taking my attention.

I clenched my fists. 'Forget about recalling the hound for a minute – what about Olivia? Have you got a healing spell back there?'

Elena turned to pull a thick book from the shelf behind her. It wasn't one I was familiar with; there was some kind of Celtic knot on the front of the leather binding.

'Can't you use that to help Norah, too?' Nicholas growled.

'Norah's not actually injured,' Elena said. 'Her life force is being drained by the hound she called, because it was sent back before it could feed. It's still bound to her – a healing spell won't do a thing.'

She found the page she was seeking. 'But this should help Olivia. It'll stop the bleeding, at least long enough to get her to a hospital.'

'It doesn't sound like a miracle cure,' I said, looking over her shoulder.

'I could probably find something more effective if I had time to look through my library.' She raised her eyebrows at me, but I shook my head.

'Olivia doesn't have that kind of time.'

'Well, this the best I've got to hand.' Elena grabbed a bowl from under the counter, propped the book against it and started pulling glass jars off shelves. 'Spells written centuries ago weren't designed for gunshot wounds, but at least we can stabilise her till the doctors take over.'

I looked at Danny. He seemed to be sticking around. 'Are you OK?' He nodded but pointed at Olivia, turning his mouth down at the corners.

'We're working on it.'

Danny hovered over the girls, his blonde head bent, wringing his hands.

Nicholas leant on the counter, holding his head and I realised that Andrews had left him with quite a nasty black eye. 'You look very piratical,' I said.

'Funny,' he replied, rolling his eyes. He handed me my crutch, then pulled me away from Elena towards the corner of the room – his hand was warm and solid on my arm. I wanted to lean into him so I shook myself free.

'Thanks for trying to stop Andrews.' I looked at the man in question, a statue in the middle of the floor. His eyes tried to follow us. I gave him the finger.

'I didn't do much,' said Nicholas, squeezing my arm. 'But I will be reviewing our hiring policy and looking very closely at anyone we've taken on this year. Who knows how many of these BRP dicks have infiltrated Ortega Enterprises.' He touched my chin and tilted my face up towards his. I held my breath, my gaze caught by his soft lips. 'So, what are you going to do?'

'Huh?' I blinked.

He jerked his chin towards Elena. 'Have you made a decision?'

'I—I can't.' Outside the room young people were partying, oblivious to what was happening behind the door. They hadn't even responded to Andrews' gunshot. It was as if they were in another world, cut off from the rest of us. How could I condemn any one of them, even if it meant closing the rift?

But Elena was right in a way, it was up to *us* – our responsibility – and so I had to make the hard choice and suffer the consequences. Before I realised I was even crying, I choked on a sob and to my surprise Nicholas wrapped his arms around me.

'You're not alone,' he whispered.

It was the first time in four years that someone had hugged me without awkwardness. I stiffened at first, then my shoulders slumped. I inhaled the lemony detergent that had been used on his shirt and the sweat he had generated carrying his sister and fighting Andrews – it wasn't a bad smell. I buried my nose in his chest and my heartbeat slowed. I hadn't realised how much I'd missed this simple human contact.

'I could save your sister,' I whispered, digging my fingers into his shirt.

'You want me to tell you what to do?' Nicholas asked. He stroked my hair and I relaxed a little more.

Mum once had a habit of doing that. In fact, she'd touched my hair when she'd left for her sister's, as if wanting to stroke it one last time. Then she'd walked away without looking back.

I wriggled and pulled free. Danny was watching us, his face unreadable.

I sighed. 'Tell me what to do, then.'

Nicholas shook his head. 'Can you really face calling that hound *here* and standing by as it spills innocent blood?'

I shook my head. 'But . . . if I don't, we'll never close the portal. Stupid teenagers will keep on calling them. Kids die either way. Just not today.'

'Leave tomorrow's problems for tomorrow. There'll be another way.' Nicholas bent his head to mine. 'There always is.'

'Like Elena said, this isn't the board room,' I stepped away from him. 'Someone isn't going to make a new deal overnight and change things. This is the situation I have to deal with, and it'll be the same tomorrow, and the day after, and the day after that.' I caught a breath.

Nicholas smiled slightly. 'I know there won't be any deals, but how do you know the rift won't eventually close by itself? It might already be smaller – has anyone measured it recently? Or, what if tomorrow someone discovers a new spell you can use? Or something else changes – maybe it turns out we *need* the magic, and the rift opened here for a reason.'

'Wishful thinking.' I said as I wrapped my arms around myself, letting the crutch knock against my knee. 'I have to deal with reality.'

'I'm just giving you alternatives to consider.'

I shook my head. 'There *are* only two alternatives – kill a bunch of kids to close the rift or walk away and leave it open . . . and put *everyone* in danger – for ever.'

Nicholas gripped my elbows. 'It's only *been* four years. Given time, people will learn to use magic more responsibly. They'll have to.' His dark eyes burned into mine. 'It'll become normal.'

'Or the BRP, or someone else, will stage a coup and use magic to control us.' I shuddered in his grip.

'It sounds as if you've made your mind up.' Nicholas retreated a pace.

I shook my head. 'Not even a little bit.'

'I'm ready.' Elena was standing in front of Olivia with a tarnished silver bowl in her hands. Steam rose from the inside and it smelt of lavender.

I hobbled to her side. 'You really believe I can do this?' I peered into the bowl. Four pieces of paper floated in a purple liquid and salt crystals were melting around them. The bowl glowed hot where Elena's skin met the metal.

'You have to . . . try . . . Ivy.' Norah looked paler than ever – she didn't need white face powder for her goth look any more.

Danny's hand hovered near mine and I smiled at him weakly. 'All right, I'll try.'

Elena took my hand. 'Repeat after me.'

I hesitated before I nodded, flooded with memories of the last time the three of us were together. The last bowl in Elena's hands had held our burning hair. I glanced again at Danny – it was as if no time at all had passed. We might have been back in the cemetery; him standing at my side. I shivered.

'Rivers shall flow: Pison, Gihon, Hedekiel and Pheat.'

I licked my lips.

'Come on . . . Ivy,' Norah whispered.

I nodded and stumbled over the unfamiliar words. Then I stopped and shook my head. 'I don't feel anything. It's not going to work.'

'You're not *trying*.' Norah looked at me with accusation on her face.

'I am and I will, but I'm telling you I haven't cast a spell right in over a year. Even if something does happen, I could make it go wrong . . . I could hurt you, Olivia.'

Olivia looked at me with eyes glazed from pain. She raised a hand – it was slick with blood. 'A risk I'm . . . willing to . . . take.' She pressed her hand back to her stomach.

I looked at Elena. 'Can you do this without me?'

Elena nodded. 'But it'll be stronger with two; doubly effective. Don't you want to help her?'

'Yes!' I wailed. And I suddenly felt, for the first time in four years, like a teenager. 'But I can't.'

A warm hand pressed down on my shoulder and when I turned, Nicholas was looking at me with steady eyes. 'You can,' he smiled at me. 'Just don't think about it too hard. When I walked into my first boardroom, I was terrified. Everybody at the meeting was at least fifteen years older than me. Most were double that.' He released a slight smile. 'They were all watching, expecting me to fail, knowing I was only there because of Dad.' He gave my shoulder a squeeze. 'I just had to pretend it wasn't important and that I was giving my presentation to Norah at home.'

'And he . . . smashed it.' Norah smiled weakly.

'So, you're saying I have to pretend this isn't important?' I frowned.

'I'm saying, find what calms you. I imagined it was just me and Norah in the room.'

'I don't . . . I don't have anyone like that.' I swallowed. 'I don't have family. Everyone left me.'

Elena's eyes flickered and she focused her attention on the bowl.

Nicholas squeezed my shoulder again. '*I'm* here. Norah and Olivia are here. Even Danny's here. No one will judge you if you can't do this.'

'Yes, they—'

'*I* won't.' Elena met my gaze. 'I understand, Ivy. Not being able to do magic freed you. I can't pretend I'd have done the same thing but if you can find a way over this block, you'll be stronger. Strong enough to close the rift maybe.'

I closed my eyes and took a deep breath. I imagined stroking Gran. My fingers in her fur. Of course, she only had fur because I'd messed up so badly. I stiffened.

Nicholas's hand moved to the back of my neck. 'Breathe, Ivy.'

I thought about my job. About the kids I'd managed to save. The ones who walked past the metal detector every day at school and glowered at me as though I was in their way. The kids who got to go home every night in one piece, because I did my job. I wasn't a dumb teenager any more. I was Ivy Elizabeth Mann. And I was good at what I did. I protected kids. And Olivia needed me right now.

I opened my eyes. '*I* calm myself,' I said. 'I'm a bad-ass. Let's do this.'

Elena exhaled. 'All right, then,' she said, and restarted the spell. '*Rivers shall flow: Pison, Gihon, Hedekiel and Pheat. But red rivers must not, they must be trapped inside her being.*'

I dutifully repeated the lines and clenched my fists to stop my hands from trembling.

Elena lowered the bowl towards Olivia's stomach and wafted the steam towards her face with one hand. I flinched as she cried out.

'*This river so red must be stopped with a golden net. Stop this blood.*'

Elena put her fingers in the bowl and flicked liquid over Olivia. Damp specks patterned her top.

Elena raised her voice. '*Hoc prohibere sanguinum.*' She looked at me.

I swallowed and then the words were tumbling out of my own mouth, a familiar sense of the inevitable starting to form. '*Hoc prohibere sanguinum.*'

Norah was mouthing the words weakly and I wanted to tell her to stop but my mouth could shape nothing but the Latin, as though the spell itself was a living thing that, once started, had to be finished. '*Hoc prohibere sanguinum.*'

I hated the feeling – *hated* it. It was just like the night Danny had died: as if the spell was saying *me*, not the other way around. But I couldn't stop, not if I wanted to save Olivia. There was a tugging – a sense of something deep inside me being dragged to the surface. '*Hoc prohibere sanguinum!*' I shouted and thrust my hands towards Olivia.

Gold flooded from my palms. It flowed over Olivia's stomach and vanished. I blinked – had I really seen that? I looked at Danny, who gave me a big thumbs up.

Norah examined Olivia and then turned her face upwards. 'I *think* it worked.'

I was shaking. I wrapped my arms around chest. 'Has the bleeding stopped?' I bent down.

'I think so,' Norah rasped.

I took a deep breath and gently moved Olivia's hand from the wound. There was still a wound where the bullet had entered, but the blood was no longer bubbling to the surface. It was as if a barrier had grown across her skin. 'The golden net,' I whispered.

Elena nodded. 'Well done.'

I stared at my hand. 'Did you see that?' My fingers looked no different. I lightly touched my chest but felt no change. I sought the feeling that had bubbled inside me, but it was gone.

Norah looked at me with a tired grin. 'Told . . . you.'

'I can still spellcast,' I muttered, my mind racing. I shook my head and touched Olivia's hand. 'How are you feeling?'

Olivia was still pale and silent, her face twisted with pain. She nodded grimly.

'We've bought her some time,' Elena said, helping me to my feet. 'Have you made a decision?'

Nicholas stepped to my side, his hand still on my shoulder. 'She's going to help Norah redo the spell.'

'I'm not!' I whirled on him.

His face was strained. He let go of me. 'You needed another option,' he said. 'And so, I came up with one.' He knelt at his sister's side and took her hands. 'Call the hound back, Norah. Let it kill *me*.' He ignored her shocked inhalation and continued. 'Then Ivy can exorcise it properly. She can break your connection with the beast and save you, and you'll have blood for your next spell.' He looked at me. 'Norah can bring Natalie back and none of the other kids will get hurt.' He offered a weak smile. 'Now that's what *I* call a win-win.'

This time I grabbed his shoulder. 'We're not doing this.'

'Yes, we are.' Nicholas rose to his feet. 'I'm *volunteering*, your conscience is clear, Ivy Mann.'

Elena was already gathering armfuls of stock from her shelves; she had the grace not to smile, but I knew from the set of the shoulders that she was triumphant.

Tears pricked my eyes. 'I don't *want* to do this.'

'It's the only way forward.' Nicholas's voice was gentle.

'Aren't you scared?' I stared into his eyes, seeking the fear. It was there – putting an edge on his gaze.

'Terrified,' he admitted ruefully. 'But it's the best way to look after my sisters . . . and you.' He forced a smile. 'If you can close that rift – well, how many people can honestly say they helped save the world?'

'But . . .' I tailed off. He was right, it was the best option. The only real option, but . . . how could I articulate what I was feeling?

He was so much more than I'd realised – honourable, intelligent, brave, dedicated to his sister. I closed my eyes. After this was over, we wouldn't have seen one another again. The Nicholas Ortega's of this world weren't friends with security guards, and they dated models and actresses. For a moment I imagined walking into a party on his arm in my tracksuit bottoms and torn shirt. There could never have been anything between us. But I didn't want to let him go.

Nicholas saw my face. He drew me towards him, turning so that my back faced the others. 'Ivy,' he started, then he cleared his throat. 'I just wanted to say . . . I've never known anyone quite like you.' He gestured to my shirt.

I snorted and folded my arms.

'And, I think you need to hear this from someone – you're impressive as hell.'

I blushed, thinking uselessly of the blood and dirt that covered me, my tangled hair and lack of make-up. 'Seriously?'

'What you've been through. What you've given up for those kids. I didn't realise before—'

'Before you had me fired?'

'Right.' His eyes flickered. 'But now I've seen you in action. I wish I could get to know you better.' He let his hand swing and touch my hip, almost a nudge. 'I think I'd have been a better person, Ivy Mann, if I'd had a friend like you.'

I looked at my toes. '*I* think you're a good person,' I mumbled.

Nicholas nudged me. 'What was that?'

'I think you're a good . . . oh!' He was smirking.

He took my hand and swallowed. 'I think we'd have had fun together, don't you?'

'I didn't think you knew the meaning of the word.' I stared at him.

'Fun?'

'Yeah.'

Nicholas winced. 'Don't know the meaning of fun? Well that's,' he paused and shook his head. 'Fair, I suppose.' He dragged a hand through his hair. 'It's my job. I have a certain image . . .'

Silence fell between us and I looked at Norah. 'Are you sure you want to do this?'

'No!' Hesitantly, as if afraid I'd cut his fingers off with Matilda, Nicholas touched my face. 'I don't want to die. I really don't want to die like this.' His good humour had vanished. 'But, for once, I haven't got a choice.'

17

'IVY!' NORAH'S VOICE made me turn. She was looking at Danny. He was standing to alert, like a dog spotting a rabbit. He saw me looking and raised a finger. I followed the line of his arm and it seemed he was trying to draw my attention to Olivia's phone. But it sat silent and still.

'What?' I frowned.

Nicholas traced the direction of my gaze then straightened. 'I think he's trying to tell us that Andrews' device is still blocking the phones. No-one can contact us, if they need to.' He strode to his immobilised ex-driver. Frustration boiled from Andrews – his muscles strained, but he still couldn't move. Nicholas reached carefully into his jacket, withdrew the device Andrews had waved at them, threw it on the ground and stamped. There was the sound of cracking glass and metal scraping on tile, then the shrill ringing of the phone behind the Emporium desk.

I jumped. We all stared at the device, as though it was an alien being beamed in. No one moved to pick it up. It stopped ringing.

'You have reached the Emporium.' Elena's voice, tinny and mechanical. '*If you have this number you are one of a privileged few. Don't abuse it.*'

'Elena? Elena, it's Dylan. Please pick up – *pick up!*' His voice, saturated with fear, whispered into the phone. 'Please, Elena. Please, oh, please!' His voice broke. 'It's my *Mum*! I did the spell you told me to do to bring her back. Oh God, please, pick up. You have to help me! She rose from the dead, but she's killed everyone – even the baby. She's eating him! Please Elena, what do I do? She's going to find me.' The boy was sobbing wildly now. 'There must be a way to send her back. *Please.*'

We kept staring at the phone, all of us frozen, listening.

'I did just what you said. I did the ritual. Those *things* came and . . . and killed a bunch of people from class. It was awful. Then I did the resurrection spell – I used the book like you said. I'm *sure* I did it right. Something's gone wrong. She's not . . . she's not Mum. I think she's like a *zombie* or something! What do I do? Norah was right – I should never have—'

Finally, Elena moved. As she reached for the phone, Dylan screamed and there was a clatter – as if the handset had dropped to the floor. We all stared, horrified, as if we could see the scene at the end of the line rather than just hear as the boy's mother found him.

Norah and Olivia had their hands over their ears by the end.

'I don't know what went wrong.' Elena put the handset back on the cradle with a shaking hand. 'He must not have—'

'What have you done? That boy said he did everything *you* told him.' I shook my head. 'You can't bring back the dead, Elena – it was the first thing we learnt.'

'*We* didn't use a blood sacrifice! He must have done it wrong!'

The phone rang again. This time Elena answered, with the tiniest tremble in her voice. 'Emporium.'

Faintly I heard the voice on the other end. Elena listened, said something with whispered urgency, then hung up the phone.

'What?' I snapped.

'That was Isobel.' She rubbed her face.

'Isobel . . . Hughes?' Norah looked up, her eyes were red-rimmed and exhausted.

'One of the others you gave the spell to, Elena?' I guessed. 'It's gone wrong for her, too.'

Elena looked away. 'She said . . . she said her dad killed her mum and now they're *both* after her. She said she was coming here, I told her not to, but she hung up.'

'Her dad killed her mum and her *mum's* after her, too? Dylan was right, they *are* zombies!' Olivia laughed bitterly then winced and gripped her stomach, silenced by pain. 'That girl's coming here . . . with *zombies*!'

Nicholas took my hand and I let him. 'This is bad.'

'Bad,' I agreed. I touched Matilda. Violet had been easy enough to stop eight years ago, but she'd been newly raised, confused and trapped inside a circle. I grimaced. 'We need fire.'

'You're not burning Emporium,' Elena snapped.

'There are *people* out there,' Olivia reminded me.

'We'll send them home.' I started for the door – Nicholas at my side. 'The party's over.'

Elena blocked our way. 'It's not easy to get in here and if there are zombies out there, those kids are probably safer where they are – don't you think?'

I stared at her for a moment. 'Maybe. We can defend the kill box.' I glanced at Nicholas. 'I assume this means you've changed your mind about being a sacrifice?'

He grimaced. 'For now. If we can't actually raise Natalie . . .'

'No more stupid ideas.' I pointed at his sister. 'Stay with Norah and Olivia. I'll go with Elena and see what kind of defence we can put together.'

'Magical zombie repellent?' Nicholas asked.

I released Matilda from her sheath. 'Good idea.'

✻ ✻ ✻

We pushed our way through the sweating bodies in the silent disco. Elena sneered as she cleared us a path, shoving headphoned dancers out of her way. She ignored the angry yells that followed us.

'Are you sure you don't want to call a hell hound?' she snapped as a lad our own age tried to get in her face. She stamped on his instep.

'Quite sure.' I showed him Matilda and the lad backed away. See, I know how to deal with people!

We reached the door – she buzzed it open and we stepped together into the kill box. The door slammed shut behind us and I jumped, gooseflesh appearing on my arms. The corridor seemed shorter than before and the wooden door to the street, the one I'd kicked in earlier, was closed ahead of us with the lock dangling from splinters. I went to prop it open.

'What are you doing?' Elena pulled her bag off her shoulder and put it between her feet.

'We need to see when they arrive, don't we?'

'CCTV.' Elena said, as if I had less sense than a Year Seven in the last week before Christmas.

'Right.' I looked back as she used her card on the single keypad, then slipped it back into the pocket of her tight leather pants.

A section of the wall peeled away to reveal a screen. 'We can watch the street from here.'

'Why were you expecting to need that?' I walked back. 'Do you spend a lot of time in this corridor?'

'I'm dealing with the BRP,' Elena said witheringly. 'The kill box is my first line of defence. And aren't you pleased you don't have to stand by an open door and watch for zombies?'

'I suppose.' I looked at the bag. 'What have you got in there?'

'Normally I'd gas anyone in the corridor trying to get in.' Elena said and cracked her knuckles. 'I'm guessing that won't work on the dead. They aren't breathing.'

'What will? If you won't let me burn them . . .'

'In here?' Her lip curled again. 'I take it *you* don't want to keep breathing either?'

'Fine then.' I folded my arms. 'What?'

'Normal incantations, like the freezing spell the girls used on Andrews, won't work,' Elena said. She knelt and started to pull things out of her bag. 'Those spells influence the mind.'

'And zombies don't have minds.'

Elena looked up. 'Exactly. Assuming our zombie lore is accurate.'

'Which we mostly got from watching *Shaun of the Dead* and *Zombieland* in your dad's basement,' I sighed and dropped my arms to my sides.

Elena's lips twitched. 'Remember how much Danny and Vi—' she hesitated. I saw her force the name through her lips. 'Violet hated those films.' Her knuckles were transparent on her bag.

I nodded, pretending I hadn't noticed how hard it was for her to talk about her girlfriend. 'She used to watch from behind three cushions.'

'And remember how she always made us turn horror films off just before the end?' Elena's smile grew unconsciously brighter. 'She said she wouldn't sleep if she saw the inevitable comeback. She wanted to go to bed believing the monster had been killed for good, even if there were three sequels.' Elena fell silent and her smile died. 'And then . . . we turned *her* into the monster.' She flicked her eyes back to mine. 'I know you were thinking it.'

I shook my head. 'Actually, I was thinking about Danny. He used to hide behind *me,* or pretend he needed more snacks, during the scariest parts. He spent half of *Resident Evil* in the kitchen eating popcorn with your dad.'

Elena snorted and the smile ghosted over her lips again. 'They were better than us.'

I nodded.

'I wonder how they'd have dealt with all of this.'

I forced myself not to comment. But I knew neither Danny nor Vi would have made the choices Elena had. 'So . . .' I said finally. 'What *are* we going to do about the zombies?'

This time Elena grinned. And suddenly we were kids again. 'Wait till you see this.'

'What?'

She gestured in front of her. 'We're going to magic the floor.'

'What, make it slippery?'

She shook her head. 'Heard of quicksand?'

I looked at the concrete beneath my feet and stamped – it was as solid as ice. 'I'm not sure . . .'

'What's concrete made from?' Elena said, as she put a bowl down in front of her. She started to shred herbs into it.

'Water, sand . . .' My smile widened. 'Oh, I see – it's a kind of reversion spell?'

Elena pulled a couple of bottles out of the bag. I didn't dare look too closely at the contents. 'Watch the alley while I finish setting it up.' She opened one of the jars and poured some liquid into the bowl. Immediately my eyes started to water as if I'd been chopping onions all day – it made it difficult to watch the screen. I rubbed my face and leant forward to focus. It was chilling, viewing a scene I'd already walked through in static black and white. Nothing moved – then a cat stalked across the picture and I jumped.

'What is it?' Elena looked up.

'Just a cat.' I rubbed my arms and then my ears, the distant growl seemed embedded in my brain now. 'Can I ask you something?'

Elena didn't answer, but she looked at me.

'When I exorcised one of the hell hounds it bit me. Is there any chance that its saliva, somehow, I don't know?' I rubbed my hands through my hair. 'When it got inside me, is it . . . connecting us somehow?'

'What do you mean?'

'I hear growling,' I said. 'The doctor says its tinnitus, because of my injuries, but it stopped when I spoke a psalm to help Norah.'

Elena froze. 'That's not good.'

'I didn't think it was.' I pinned my eyes back to the screen. 'I just wondered if you'd heard . . .'

Elena shook her head. 'I've never read about anyone surviving a hell hound attack. Anyone ever bitten has been torn apart moments later. I don't know what you're hearing, maybe it'll wear off.'

'Yeah.' I shook my head. 'It isn't important right now anyway. How long do you think it'll take Isobel to get here? Where does she live?'

'Hammersmith, I think.' Elena said, turning back to her preparations. 'It depends if she managed to get on the Tube—'

'If she did, she'll be all right!' Tension fled my shoulders. 'They won't be able to follow her.'

Elena's smile had vanished. She shook her head. 'It's like Norah and the hell hounds, Ivy. Her parents will be connected to Isobel, as long as she's alive. Even if she loses them on the Tube . . . she'll still lead them here.' Elena's eyes chilled me.

'Through London,' I said, slowly. 'Through *rush-hour* in London!'

Elena had the grace to look miserable. 'There's nothing we can do except stop them here and hope they're too focused on Isobel to be . . .'

'Hungry?'

'Well . . . yeah.'

'We have to call the police,' I groaned. 'They need to know what's coming.'

'*Don't!*'

'Shut up, Elena.' I dialled and put my phone to my ear.

A voice replied immediately. 'Nine-nine-nine, what service do you require— ambulance, fire, police or coastguard?'

I paused. 'All of them?'

159

'You realise this is your fault,' I said coldly, putting my phone away and turning back to the screen.

Behind me, Elena said nothing.

'They only believed me because calls had already started coming in. There have been attacks all along the District Line route.'

Elena maintained her silence.

'People have died, Elena.'

Her shoulders, curved over the bowl, shuddered, 'It'll be worth it,' she said, eventually.

'Worth it?' I froze.

'If we can put Danny back in his body, we can close the rift. Nothing like this can ever happen again.'

I took hold of the screen with shaking hands. 'Why are you *really* doing this? Trying to raise Danny – is it just to close the rift?'

For a long moment Elena made no answer. She continued mixing the stinking mess in the bowl, then sat back with her head bowed. 'You think I didn't care that Danny died? He was your boyfriend, sure, but he was my best friend – like Violet was yours.' I blinked, and she finally looked up at me – her blue eyes cloudy with regret. I stepped backwards, shocked at the expression on her face. 'Afterwards . . . I couldn't *face* coming back to find you. It wasn't just that I couldn't forgive you for killing Violet—'

'We've covered this.'

Elena shook her head. 'Deep down, I *knew* it was more my fault than yours, but how could I face that? How could I face *you*, knowing Danny was dead and it was my fault? That Violet had killed him . . . like that . . .' she tailed off. 'It was easier to blame *you*.'

She shook her head. 'But if I can bring Danny back, it turns it back, doesn't it? Makes it right?'

'I . . . I don't know.' I knelt beside her. 'Doing all of this, it's just piling wrong on top of wrong.' Carefully, I touched her balled fists. '*Neither* of us could have known that crazy spell would work,' I said. 'So maybe neither of us is to blame. We were kids, *E*, grieving kids and something horrible happened to us. It wasn't anyone's fault, not really.'

'Maybe it wasn't our fault,' she said, and her shoulders dropped as if a mass had been shifted from them. 'But it *is* our responsibility.' I nodded, and she laid her own hand over mine and we sat together, hands growing warmer.

After a while I caught her eye. 'Raising Danny,' I started. 'You know it can't be done.' I was beyond tired. My legs were going to sleep as if my body had decided to stop waiting for me to make the sensible decision, and the words were hard to say but Elena needed to hear them. 'All that those other kids managed to do was raise revenants, like we did with Vi. So, it couldn't be innocent blood that's needed to make the ritual work. You were wrong, can't you see that?'

Elena tugged her hands abruptly from mine, shaking her head. 'None of them were as strong as Norah Ortega – she's a nuclear power station, Ivy! If we can just get her to cast the spells—'

'Why won't you give up?' I defied my legs and leapt to my feet, shoving Elena hard. The bowl she had been filling spilt. Noxious yellow gas boiled over the floor.

'You idiot!' Elena fumbled for the *Necronomicon*. 'We'll have to cast *now*.' She flicked to a page near the middle.

I covered my mouth; the smell was even worse now – onions

and Sulphur – like kitchen bins in hell. 'We can't. Isobel isn't here yet.' I turned stubbornly back to my view of the alley and the cat standing at the doorway as if waiting to be let in.

'I don't have any more of these ingredients,' Elena snapped. 'If the vapour vanishes, we won't be able to cast at all.' She spun me around and stood toe-to-toe. 'You're happy for whatever's chasing her to get in?' She jabbed a finger into my chest. 'You said it yourself, there are *hundreds* of kids behind us.'

'There has to be another w—' I started.

'There isn't.' Elena hesitated. 'We'll tell Isobel to jump when she gets here. You can catch her.' Elena gestured towards the rising smog. 'I *can* do this on my own, but it'll be a stronger spell with two of us – a better trap.'

I rubbed my arms. 'Fine, but if that kid gets hurt because of this . . .' She was already picking up the *Necronomicon*.

'Read it with me.' Elena held the book out. There was a sheet of paper on top of the spell, an English translation, or most of one. I scanned the words then nodded. We spoke together quickly, as the gas dissipated across the floor.

'The oak to the acorn, the sea to the stream,
The night to the morning, the cheese to the cream,
Feel what you once were, be what you once were.
By Arianrhod I command it. By Cailleach I demand it.
By Cerridwen and Gwyddion I compel it.
Become what you once were: Quod cum esset facti.
Sand in the stone: In harenae lapis
Quod cum esset facti, in harenae lapis.
Quod cum esset facti, in harenae lapis.'

I felt that strange tugging sensation in my chest and closed my eyes. When I opened them, the gas had vanished and the bowl was empty. Nothing had changed.

'It didn't work . . .' I started. Then I realised that the floor in front of us, while still concrete grey, had an odd glitter to it. I took a careful step forward and poked Matilda into the ground. Instead of meeting resistance Matilda sank, and fine powder puffed around the blade. Off balance I tipped forward and Elena grabbed me. 'Careful!'

I regained my feet and moved backwards. 'Is the whole floor like that?'

Elena nodded. 'I hope so.'

'How deep is it?'

'Deep . . . I hope.'

I exhaled. 'Tell me there's a back way out of this place.'

There was a noise outside and I turned back to the monitor. The cat was caterwauling now and batting at the door, demanding to be allowed in. The door was shuddering slightly, held closed only by its own weight.

'Is that your c—' I started, then I stared. There was something very familiar about that animal. But it couldn't be. There were thousands of fat tabbies in London. As I stared, persuading myself that I had to be wrong, a teenage girl staggered into view. The monochrome screen painted the blood on her face black and she weaved from side-to-side as if she'd run a marathon, her legs barely able to hold her.

'That must be Isobel.' I pointed to the screen.

'Is she alone?' Elena asked grimly, flicking to another page in the horrible spell book.

'Ye—' I stopped. Because she wasn't alone.

I felt Elena's gaze on me but couldn't tear my eyes from the screen. Behind Elena appeared a woman wearing yoga pants and a once white T-shirt. The front of the T-shirt was soaked with black blood and the front of her throat was missing. She moved with the kind of strange jerky speed that I remembered from the moment Violet killed Danny, as if she was stronger than she had been, but her muscles weren't completely under her control. Or, as if she had to think about each movement – the chemistry it took to make every muscle expand or contract – before she made it.

The moment she appeared on screen the cat, which had been so determined to get inside, streaked off behind an overflowing bin.

I could hear sounds from the alley now – Isobel's gasping sobs and a bubbling hiss from the woman as air rasped in and out of her mangled throat. Instinctively I lurched towards the door. Elena grabbed me just in time. 'Don't!' She pointed to the floor.

I set my jaw and gripped Matilda in one hand, my crutch in the other. Then I turned back to the screen. There was a man on there now, still wearing the suit he had been buried in, grave dirt in his hair and on his face. His chin and hands shone with gore. His mouth was open. He was groaning, almost crooning, as if calling his daughter's name.

'It's them,' I whispered. 'Her parents.'

The door slammed open, bouncing once more from the frame, and Isobel staggered in. Her pale blonde hair was unkempt and she was wearing her school blazer. Sweat glued her blouse to her chest.

'Stop!' Elena yelled.

Shocked, Isobel halted and lifted her glazed, exhausted gaze to Elena's. 'Help me!'

I pushed past Elena. 'The floor's not safe, you have to jump.'

Isobel blinked, as though finding my words hard to process.

'Jump, Isobel!' I demanded. Automatically she took a couple of steps backwards, to give herself a run up. I raised my hand to stop her, but it was too late . . . Isobel had stepped into her mother's reach.

I cried out, harmonising with Isobel's scream of terror. Her mother's mouth opened inhumanly wide as she dug her fingers into her daughter's neck. Her teeth were bloodstained. Then Isobel's father joined them. He grabbed hold of Isobel's outstretched arm, but she tore herself free of both. She hurtled towards Elena and me, leaping as high as she could, but her father caught her leg.

Elena hooked three of Isobel's fingers. For a moment she hung between Elena and her parents. I stared past the horrifying tableau. 'Elena!' I gasped.

Elena glanced up – the alleyway was no longer empty; there had to be a dozen Londoners in front of the building. To all intents and purposes, the people were dead; the injuries they had sustained would allow nothing else. At least one looked as if he had been hit by a car, trailing a broken leg. Others had torn-off faces or ripped out throats, like Isobel's mother. Two or three had been eviscerated, and they moved with guts dangling from gaping wounds. They all lurched towards Isobel with a single-minded purpose and uncanny speed.

'I'm slipping!' Isobel was sobbing. 'Don't let go.' Her blue eyes were wide and blank with fear.

I lunged to try and reach Isobel's other hand, then I remembered the crutch now dangling from my elbow. 'Take this.' I swung it up towards her. She grasped the end with her free hand, shrieking.

Her father was gnawing on her calf and her mother was trying to push past him to reach her.

'Elena, get him off her,' I yelled, hauling on the crutch.

'*Incensa.*' Elena yanked one of her hands free of Isobel's grip and thrust it towards the monster on the girl's leg. She shouted again and then a third time. The third shout was accompanied by a gout of fire that spat from her palm and into his face.

The heat of the flame singed Isobel's hair.

'I thought you said—'

'Shut *up*, Ivy.'

As he burned, Isobel's father squirmed until he was forced to release his daughter. Isobel slammed forward, disappearing into the floor with a shocked gasp and a puff of dust. The weight of her still dangled from my crutch and I started to pull. 'Elena, help! She'll suffocate!'

Elena leant over me and grabbed the end of the crutch, she added her strength to mine and we hauled Isobel on to solid ground. She flopped, on to the concrete, choking and sobbing. She was spitting grey dust and bleeding from half a dozen wounds.

I checked that she was alive and then looked up at the zombies. They hadn't stopped coming. First was Isobel's mother. She pushed past the charred husk that had been her husband and dropped into the sand with no hesitation.

'What the ...?' I gaped.

'They can't think,' Elena rasped, dragging Isobel to her feet. 'They've still got the compulsion to come after her.'

'What about those others?' I pointed to the group outside the alleyway. 'She didn't raise them, did she? Does the spell still—'

'*I* don't know!' Elena dragged her fingers through her hair, making it stand up crazily. 'Maybe they're compelled to follow their makers?'

I stared in horror as the first of the zombies found the door – a businessman, going by his attire. He was slender and long fingered, as if he'd spent his evenings playing tennis or the piano. His shirt was ragged, and his chest looked like an alien had burst from it – shards of ribs protruded and there was a bloody mess where unblemished skin should be.

I caught my breath as he just kept rocking forward, pitching without complaint into the sand.

He was followed by the greatest horror yet. A mum with a baby sling still cinched to her front. The baby had arms and legs, but no head. The mum had been caught from behind – she looked almost normal from the front, until you saw her chin still dripping with her own child's blood.

I covered my mouth as revulsion spilled from me and I retched. She reeled straight into the sand and, to my relief, vanished. Over and over the zombies walked soundlessly into the pit, unable to make sense of what had happened to those ahead of them.

'Let's go.' I stood and pulled Isobel with me. Her hand was clammy with sweat and blood. She must have held on to the crutch through sheer willpower. I felt a shiver of respect for her.

'Go?' Isobel turned a shocked gaze on to me, her pupils dilated and vibrating.

'Those *things* will be trapped in here. We'll get out through the Emporium.'

Elena opened her mouth to answer then stopped, looking past me. The next zombie was a gangly teenaged boy wearing a blue baseball cap. He staggered into the sand but when the powder reached his waist, he stopped falling. Immediately he began to pull himself forward, as if through a low tide, his mouth open – hissing intently – eyes on Isobel.

'What's happening?'

'The hole's full,' Elena swallowed.

'Burn it then.' Isobel grabbed her arm. 'Do what you did before.'

Reluctantly, Elena held out her hand. '*Incensa. Incensa. Incensa!*'

As before, her fist became a flame thrower and the boy was transformed into a human torch. The smell of burning flesh and charring polyester turned the corridor into the barbecue from hell.

I pressed my hand harder to my mouth. 'Come on.' I dragged Isobel towards the inner door, as more zombies stepped into the smoking pit and continued coming.

Elena threw fire at them, but it was as if she had an oil reservoir inside, that was running low. Each flame spurted with less strength until, finally, she dropped her arm. Her narrow face was gaunt, as though she hadn't eaten for a week. She looked almost as bad as Norah.

I stood at the console with Isobel. 'How do I—?'

Elena reached over me, pressed her hand to the screen and the inner door cracked open. I was about to pull Isobel through when our way was blocked by a stream of tired teenagers in club gear. The silent disco was over.

18

I RISKED A GLANCE behind us – the first zombie was clambering out of the pit, scratching at the concrete with the sound of nails on a chalkboard.

'Out of the way!' Elena yelled. But now that the DJ had called time, the crowd of dancers was determined to push in one direction – the exit. They were laughing and joking, shoving one another, glitter-eyed with excitement. I supposed many of them needed to get home before parents demanded to know where they'd been.

'Let us through!' Elena growled, but she was ignored. Sweating, hormonal teens pressed forwards, giggling, gasping for fresh air, commenting on the music, or on this or that outfit, or hottie, checking their phones, sliding oyster cards from wallets.

'Stop!' I cried, terrified for them. I raised one fist above me.

'Incensa. Incensa. *Incensa!*' Fire scorched the ceiling above their heads. Young people wailed – some started to fight backwards, while others continued to shove forwards. With some difficulty, I fought nausea and managed to stay on my feet. No wonder Elena looked so wiped out; that spell had drawn on my own energy, my own inner fire. She must have burned through most of hers.

I raised my hand again. '*Stop!*' I was about to put my body through another round of the incantation when Isobel's scream drew my attention. I spun to see that a dead businessman had pulled himself completely out of the pit. His claw-like hands were wrapped around her throat.

I whirled and brought Matilda down hard. She sliced through the man's arms as if they were made of cake. Good girl, Matilda. Twitching limbs thudded to the floor between us and the zombie staggered.

Behind him, more were coming. The pit was full of bodies with heads and shoulders poking from the powder, like buried treasure unearthed by the tide.

'Turn it back!' I called.

'What?' Elena clutched Isobel with one hand and the *Necronomicon* with the other.

'We have to turn the floor back into concrete.'

'I don't think . . .' Elena shook her head. 'I don't have any more ingredients . . . my bowl.' I followed her stare; the bowl had been kicked into a far corner.

'We're not casting a new spell.' I shook her shoulder. 'We're *reversing* this one.'

Elena nodded, flipped pages frantically and then held the spell up to me.

I looked at it, mentally transposing as best I could. I'd done things like this before. I hadn't thought of it as casting magic, just switching off a hex – like turning a radio from the correct frequency. 'All right, follow me this time:'

Elena nodded.

I spoke as slowly as I dared.

'The acorn to the oak, the stream to the seas,
The morning to the night, the cream to the cheese,
Feel what you once were, be what you once were.
By Arianrhod I command it. By Cailleach I demand it.
By Cerridwen and Gwyddion I compel it.
Become what you once were: Quod cum esset facti.
Stone out of sand'

I hesitated.

'What is it?' Elena yelled.

'I'm not great at Latin. Give me a minute.'

'We don't have a minute.' She screamed.

Another zombie was pulling himself out of the pit, his chest was already on the concrete in front of me.

Isobel caught my arm. 'What do you need to say?'

I held my crutch in front of me, trying to push the zombie back into the powder. 'The spell says *sand in the stone*, but I need to say *stone out of sand.*'

Isobel pulled out her phone. 'Siri: English to Latin translation.' Her voice was trembling, and it was noisy, but somehow Siri understood.

'Clever girl!' Elena grabbed the phone from her as Google appeared. She typed quickly then held the phone up to me.

'*Lapis de harenae lasarpici-feris.*' I read, still poking the zombie desperately in the face.

Elena nodded. '*Quod cum esset facti, Lapis de harenae lasarpiciferis.*

Quod cum esset facti, Lapis de harenae lasarpiciferis.'

The tugging was a welcome sensation this time, my chest expanded and contracted. Then the zombie I had been fending off made a choking sound and stopped moving towards me. He twisted and yanked but was unable to pull himself free. Another was stuck at the far end of the floor, one foot sunk to the ankle in the concrete.

A yowl assailed my ears and there was a streak of tabby fur. The cat I had seen earlier leapt from trapped head to trapped head, then blurred past me and into the crowd of teenagers with a wail. 'What are you standing there for? Stupid girl!'

'*Gran?*' I swayed and caught myself on the crutch. Three more zombies were on her tail and now they had a solid, if lumpy, floor to stagger over.

The nearest teens had seen the attack on Isobel. Now they were backing away furiously. The crowd pushed back against them for a moment, then whispers and fear spread like an oil spill – the tide turned and suddenly the teenagers were racing back into the building. I wasted no time hauling Elena and Isobel after them, then turning and slamming the door on a scrabbling hand. There was a clunk as the magnetic locks engaged. I stepped backwards, shaking as thuds and thumps rained on the metal.

I looked at Elena. 'Where *is* the back way out of this place?'

Elena shook her head. She hugged the *Necronomicon*. 'There's only one way in and out.'

'But . . . fire regulations,' I gasped.

Elena shrugged. 'I didn't want anyone sneaking into Emporium.'

'You—' I stopped and swiped a hand across my eyes. 'We didn't send those kids home. You said they'd be *safer* in here.'

'We couldn't have known how many zombies—' Elena started.

'No, but you knew there wasn't a back way out.' I tilted my head at her. 'You didn't want them to go, did you? You wanted them here, in case Norah decided to cast her spell.'

Elena didn't answer.

Isobel sobbed beside me and I tightened my jaw. 'Never mind,' I ground out. 'That door's strong. It's holding. Let's get back to the others.'

It wasn't that easy. Hundreds of teenagers had turned from feisty youths, determined to skip school and party, into terrified children who wanted nothing more than an adult to save them. We weren't really adults, but we were among the oldest there and that seemed to be enough.

'What's happening? . . . Can you get us out of here? . . . You were out there, weren't you, what's going on? . . . Can you help us? . . . What *were* those things? . . . I want my—'

I gave up trying to push my way back to Elena's shop. I looked for the DJ booth – it wasn't far. I used the threat of Matilda to clear us a path to the compartment, scowled at the dreadlocked DJ who was behind the screen obliviously packing up his equipment, then signalled to Elena to give me a boost. She frowned but helped me climb on top of the cubicle.

I waved Matilda in one hand and my crutch in another. 'Quiet!'

To my surprise the kids shut up – desperate for a voice of authority, I guess.

173

'I know you're scared.' I looked at the sea of pale faces; groups of friends clinging to one another, holding hands, or hugging. A few held their phones up as if recording me would make them safer, putting an extra layer of padding between themselves and reality. There was still baby fat in their cheeks, and few had any facial hair. Their eyes were wide and shocked. These were the people we had put in danger all those years ago. These were the ones I had to protect.

'My name's Ivy,' I called. 'There's been a lot going on out there this afternoon. I expect most of you have missed calls from your parents.'

Eyes went to phones. Suddenly those nagging parents seemed like lifelines. I could hardly remember what that was like.

'Don't call them back just yet,' I shouted, as fingers started to move over screens.

'Why not?' It was the girl with the bright purple hair, the one who'd wanted drugs. She looked a lot sharper now – scared sober.

'You *can*, just give me a minute of quiet first.' I saw movement at the back of the room. Nicholas had opened the door to Emporium and was standing in the entrance, watching and listening. I gave him a kind of half-smile. He offered a wave in return. Gran slithered between his legs like a furry snake and vanished into the room. I'd deal with her next. 'I know some of you saw what was happening in the corridor.' I glanced at Elena and the shuddering Isobel.

'Zombies!' a boy shouted.

'Don't be a moron!' Someone else yelled.

'He's right,' I thudded my crutch on the hollow roof. 'There are basically zombies out there. The first ones were raised by someone doing a *very* stupid spell.' I struggled not to look at Isobel – who knew what they'd do to her if they thought it was her fault? 'But it seems to be spreading just like in the old films – someone gets killed by a zombie and, assuming the brain is intact, they come back as one too.'

'How?' The speaker was androgynous – peroxide shoulder length hair brushed back from a sharp face. Trousers and a waistcoat. Strapped breasts, or no breasts, I couldn't tell. It didn't matter.

'I don't know,' I shrugged. 'How does anything like this work? Magic, I guess.' I looked out at the expectant faces.

'Why are they *here*?'

I was hoping they wouldn't ask that. I didn't want to lie to them. 'That's not important. The important thing is, how do we stop them? How many of you have tried to cast spells?'

About half the hands went up. Some of the faces were surprised – people edged away from friends.

'How many of you found they worked well for you?'

The teenagers with their hands up looked at one another and hands started to go down until about ten remained, including the androgyne, a pair of Chinese twins, a stunning black girl and the boy who had shouted 'zombies' earlier. 'All right.' I nodded, somewhat relieved. I hadn't been expecting even that many. 'You lot come here – we're going to find a way to defend ourselves if they come through that door.'

It was already shuddering.

'What about *us*?' A group of lads, toughness returning. 'If there are zombies, we want weapons.'

I looked around us. The room was basically empty, but there

was some furniture along the walls. 'If you can break that up and make yourselves weapons, then do it!'

'What about that?' One of the lads pointed at Matilda. 'You should give it to us – I bet you can't use it anyway!'

I glowered. 'You can have Matilda if you can take her,' I put her back in her sheath. 'But you'd be better with a chair leg – that way you won't cut your own hand off!'

'Hey!'

I ignored him. 'The rest of you, stay away from that end of the room.' I pointed at the quaking door. 'Call your parents if you like, but don't tell them to come and get you – you know what they'll be walking into. If you love them, ask them to stay home and wait.'

'But . . . I want my Mum.' It was a child's cry and it broke my heart.

'You'll see her soon.' I hesitated, but there was nothing else to say. I jumped down from the DJ booth and Elena caught me as I stumbled, my crutch sliding out from under me.

'Hey!' The DJ called, 'Were you serious just then?'

'Deadly.' I looked at his horrified face. 'Sorry.'

Elena steadied me and I looked at Isobel. She was crying, huge silent tears mingling with thick streams of snot. She wiped her wrist over her face, but the tears kept coming. 'My mum's dead,' she whispered.

I nodded. 'You messed up.' She gasped, and I looked hard at Elena. 'But it wasn't your fault.'

'That's right.' Isobel stared at up at Elena. 'I did what *you* told me.' She hobbled away from her, favouring her injured leg, and I caught her with one hand.

'Come on, let's get you sat down.'

I headed towards Nicholas.

'What should I—' Elena started.

'You like telling teens how to cast spells,' I snapped. 'Get that lot doing *Incensa*.'

'We can't burn them in here,' Elena reminded me. 'The whole place could go up.'

I pointed to the book that she still clutched like a baby. 'Well, I know there are spells in there you can use.'

✳ ✳ ✳

Nicholas watched me shuffle through the crowd towards him, Isobel in tow. The kids let us pass this time, more focused on their phones than on me. Groups of girls were crying together. I saw more than one gang of lads doing the same thing.

'You did a good job calming them down,' Nicholas said as I drew near.

'Did I?' I looked behind me. A lot of the kids were sitting now, arms over bent shoulders and heads together. Some of the boys were smashing tables and chairs, hefting splintered shafts or bent metal poles. There was a scatter-gun of out-of-place laughter, that quickly stopped. A few sat around the edges of the room staring into space.

Near the vibrating door, the ten who'd admitted to having magical skills gathered around Elena and the *Necronomicon*. I just hoped Elena had found something useful and not too dangerous to teach them.

'How are Norah and Olivia?' I asked, looking past him.

'Hanging on,' Nicholas replied, but his voice was grim. I touched his arm – the warmth of his skin through his shirt was a comfort I mustn't start to depend on. I pulled myself free and strode into the shop. Andrews remained standing to attention. Danny seemed to be browsing the shelves, his feet about an inch above the floor. Norah and Olivia were lying side by side using Nicholas's bag as a pillow.

Gran was curled in the crook of Norah's arm, purring softly.

I directed Isobel to sit beside Norah. She collapsed gratefully to the floor in a pile of school uniform and put her head in her hands. Her hair fell over her face and her shoulders started to shake.

'What are you doing here, Gran?' I crouched beside the cart. 'In case you haven't noticed, it's dangerous.'

Gran stopped purring and glowered at me through narrowed green eyes. 'I came to *help*,' she said caustically. 'You kids are always screwing things up! And you need someone to look after you.'

I thought about arguing, then realised that she couldn't leave now even if she wanted to and sighed. 'It's good to see you,' I said instead.

'Obviously.' Gran cocked her chin at Norah. 'What did you do to the girl?'

'It wasn't me! Her life force is linked to the hound she called.' I allowed myself to slide down the wall and on to my butt. 'It's draining her to get back to this plane.'

'Using her own energy to hunt her – that's dogs for you.' Gran sneered. 'Nasty.' She nudged her head under Norah's hand until the girl weakly rubbed her ears. 'What are you going to do about it?'

I leant my head on the wall. 'I've got a zombie horde trying to get in, a frozen BRP shill to deal with, Olivia and Isobel both need a hospital . . .' I stopped. 'There's no right answer here . . . I don't know.'

Norah opened her eyes and met mine. I stared into them shamefacedly. Then she nodded and closed them.

Nicholas came to sit beside me. He let his fingers fall so that they touched mine and I smiled a little.

'What happened out there?' he asked after a moment.

'Zombies.' I didn't move my head – staring at the ceiling as I spoke. 'Dozens of them. We stopped a lot, but there are more trying to get in – they're after Isobel like the hound is after Norah.'

'*Actual* zombies?' He shifted so that he was looking at me. I dropped my eyes. His were warm brown but skeptical.

I sighed. 'Yep. Movie zombies, with a hunger for flesh. They're faster than you'd think.'

'I don't feel so good,' Isobel whispered. She raised a tear-streaked face and I put the back of my wrist on her forehead, just as I remembered Mum doing when I was little.

'You're burning up.'

'I feel sick.'

Instantly Gran was up and streaking across the room. 'Stay away from me! Do you know how I have to wash this fur?'

There was a display of bowls above our heads. I rose and took one down. It seemed to be gold-plated. Good. 'If you need to throw up – do it in here.'

Danny had floated nearer, he was watching Isobel with a concerned gaze.

'Nothing else I can do,' I said to him, sadly. 'She needs a doctor too.'

Danny nodded.

I looked at Nicholas. 'You'll be needing a weapon.'

He indicated a bulge in his trouser pocket. 'Andrews' gun.'

'OK.'

He reached across me and tucked stray hairs behind Norah's ear. 'It's like Natalie all over again,' his voice broke.

'Come on.' I pulled him to his feet – his palm was smooth and warm in mine. 'Let's see how Elena's doing.'

He hesitated. 'I don't want to leave Norah.'

'I understand,' I replied, releasing his hand.

'But I can't just sit and watch either.' He ran his fingers through his hair, mussing it. 'I'm a terrible brother. If I'd been there for her after Natalie died, I'd have known what she was planning and stopped her. But I threw myself into work. This is my fault.' Devastation darkened his eyes.

'Where's your father?' I snapped before I could cry sympathetic tears. 'He wasn't there for her either, was he?'

Nicholas looked away. 'She's always been my responsibility.'

'Why? Is she your kid?' I shook my head. 'Your dad's the one who had her, then abandoned her. He's the ones who should be offering to die for her, not you.'

'*He's* not here,' Nicholas growled.

'Exactly my point,' I sighed. 'You can't blame yourself.'

Nicholas was quiet for a moment – he kept his eyes on mine. 'These kids aren't your responsibility either, are they?' he said. 'You didn't give birth to even one of them. Where are *their* parents?'

'That's different,' I said, turning my gaze away. 'This is my job.'

'You don't *have* a job,' Gran called from underneath the counter.

'Thanks for the reminder, Gran.' I tightened my grip on the crutch.

Nicholas stepped nearer. 'There's more to it, isn't there? Elena said you were all there when the rift was opened. Is that true? *Did* you open the rift?' He tilted my chin right and left, looking at my face with a frown. With a sinking heart, I let him. 'I thought you looked familiar. You were all over the news. Someone died.' He jolted and looked at Danny. 'It was him. He was the boy who died – Daniel Masters.'

Danny spread his hands and shrugged.

I twisted my chin from his grip. 'Yes, it *was* me. Elena and Danny too. Our best friend, Violet, was killed in a hit and run. We were trying to bring her back. Well . . . not really . . . Elena hadn't been allowed to go to the funeral, and we thought we could do a ritual to bring her closure or something. She'd found this book and we . . . it was . . . not a *laugh*, but not serious. We were *children*. We were drunk and . . . somehow it worked. We tore open this rift and since then every death or injury caused by magic is our fault. Danny was dead and Elena ran away. Who else was going to protect the kids?'

Nicholas drew back from me.

'We had no way of knowing what would happen—' I started, but then I stopped. That wasn't the point.

Gran yowled suddenly and there was a crash from outside. Teenagers started to scream. I heard Elena's raised voice – 'Now!' and then the sound of chanting.

'They're through!' I raced to the doorway, leapt over the threshold into the main room and slammed it shut behind me. The door opened behind me and I turned to see Nicholas flicking the safety catch off Andrews' gun. 'I hope you can use that thing,' I said grimly, unsheathing Matilda.

'We'll find out, won't we?' Nicholas held the gun in both hands and trained it towards the other side of the room.

Zombies were flooding in – more than I'd seen earlier. They'd broken through the metal door by using sheer weight of numbers to shatter the frame. Most of the teenagers were cowering against the back wall. There was a line of the tougher boys and girls in front of them holding chair legs and snapped pieces of railing, their faces grim. In front of *them*, were the ten practising magic users and Elena.

At least a dozen mangled zombies were leaping into the maw of two incantations. Five of the teens held their hands out and a howling wind forced the zombies back, toppling them like skittles. The other five were holding hands and chanting. A shimmering lilac wall appeared around them and pushed the tumbling zombies back towards the doorway. It formed a barrier between the creatures and the rest of the room.

'How long will that hold?' I yelled.

Elena looked towards the sound of my voice. 'As long as they've got the energy to hold it.'

'Where are the damned cavalry?' I muttered.

'The police?' Nicholas frowned.

'I called them from the corridor.' I kept Matilda in my hand but turned back towards Emporium just as Gran darted through the door.

'Ivy, come quick! There's something wrong with Is—'

A crash and a scream. Nicholas shoved me out of the way and raced back into the room. 'Norah!'

I followed as fast as I could.

19

OLIVIA WAS SITTING up, one hand on her stomach and the other held out in front of her. She was chanting a version of the wind spell that Elena had taught the kids outside, her face wracked with agony. Blood was seeping from her wound.

The smell hit me before my eyes could take in any more; it was the ripe stench of vomit, overlaid with coppery blood and something so rancid that I covered my mouth. I blinked as I tried to take in everything at once.

Danny was standing over a barely conscious Norah, making himself as intimidating as a sixteen-year-old boy with no substance possibly could. A display of decorative knives had been knocked over and the blades were scattered on the floor beside them.

Andrews still stood in the centre of the room, so there was no danger from him. I followed the line of Olivia's pointing hands. Isobel was pinned to a wall, struggling like a bug against the wind – she was snarling, and her eyes were glazed with a yellow film. Blood-flecked vomit decorated the front of her blouse. She wasn't the teenaged girl I'd saved. She'd been infected – another thing the movies had right.

Nicholas stood off to one side – gun shaking in his hand. He raised it towards Isobel, but the muzzle wavered, and I knew he would never shoot her.

I started into the room too late. Olivia gasped and dropped her arm. Isobel shot forward as if fired from a cannon, using the wall like a gymnast with a springboard. But instead of heading towards Olivia, she threw herself at the largest, and most defenceless, target . . . Andrews.

I turned, as if in slow motion, to see the widening of his eyes and the straining of his muscles as he fought desperately to lift his arms. There was nothing he could do. Isobel slammed into him, already opening her mouth.

'*Regelo!*' I screamed, raising one hand.

Abruptly freed from the spell that had been holding him, Andrews moved faster than I would have believed possible. He threw himself backwards and simultaneously jammed his elbow under Isobel's chin, shoving her face away. She fought to reach his throat with hands like claws and he lay beneath her, holding her squirming body back.

'Don't let her bite him,' Olivia gasped. 'She's infected.'

I dived after Isobel who was screeching wordlessly, her jaw snapping.

Nicholas shouted incoherently, the gun in his hand still

shaking. His finger was nowhere near the trigger.

'I don't want to do this,' I cried as I reached them. 'I really, *really* don't want to.' I raised Matilda.

'Ivy, no!' Gran bounded towards me, but what else could I do? I dealt the most merciful blow I could. Putting all my strength into the swing, I reminded myself that this thing wasn't Isobel any more and cut her head off.

The moment her skull bounced on the ground, Isobel's body slumped and stopped moving. Thankfully her long hair had formed into a tangle over her face but blood spurted gruesomely from her neck, coating Andrews' throat and face. 'Don't let any of that get in your mouth,' Nicholas said with a strange calm. 'The infection must spread via bodily fluids.'

I turned to see him, face pale and swaying slightly, the gun still pointing at Isobel. 'You can put that down now,' I said gently.

He lowered his arm. 'You killed her.'

'She was already dead.' Olivia answered for me. 'She was dead the moment she was bitten.'

I nodded. 'I should have known . . . I mean every zombie film ever made—'

'Life isn't a movie.' Gran stalked past me to sit once more between the girls. She didn't look at me and that hurt. 'You couldn't have known.'

I nodded and turned to Andrews. He pushed Isobel's body to one side and sat up.

'Are you going to be a dick?' I asked, tilting my head to one side. 'I only ask because I don't want to deal with you *and* a horde of bloodthirsty zombies.'

Andrews shook his head, wiping his face with his jacket.

'My people should be happy enough with a zombie invasion. If they can't spin an anti-government riot out of that, then—'

Nicholas was raising the gun before I could say another word. 'Say that again!'

'*Nicholas*,' I said warningly.

'You're a . . . monster!' It was Norah's voice. I jolted in surprise and for a moment I thought she was talking about me. Isobel's tainted blood still slid from Matilda's blade, dripping into a pattern on the tiles between my feet. I *was* a monster. I swallowed. Then I realised she was talking to Andrews. She struggled out of her jacket. 'Here,' she pushed it towards me. 'You should . . . cover her.'

I took the jacket and draped it over Isobel's head. It was long enough to reach the top of her shoulders. I paused, kneeling beside her and then stood again to address Andrews. 'Get out there and help Elena hold them off,' I said to him with only the slightest tremble in my voice. 'Or Nicholas will use that gun.'

Andrews stood slowly. Isobel's blood streaked his face. He turned to the doorway.

'Wait,' I said.

He stopped.

'Did you know her?' I pointed at the body on the floor. 'She was one of the kids your lot set up, so . . . did you have like a file on her. Do you know her face? Her history?'

Andrews' jaw was set. 'I . . . know who she was,' he said eventually.

'Isobel was grieving for the loss of her father and you *used* her. Are you OK with what happened to her?' I shuffled closer to him. 'Think carefully!'

'We knew there would be collateral damage,' he said. He looked at me and to my surprise there was guilt in his eyes. Maybe he wouldn't find it so easy to live with after all. 'But it's for the greater good.' He sighed. 'The BRP are the only ones who can save us – we *should* be regulating magic users and organising spells and incantations like any other resource. We're the *only* country with magic. Think what we could be doing for ourselves.'

'Get out,' I said. 'Go on – find a way to help.'

He started for the door, just as the screaming started up again. A moment later Elena appeared in the entrance, panting wildly. 'The kids are exhausted,' she gasped. The Chinese twins were behind her, holding their arms out. They had cleared her a path. Even as she spoke, they collapsed into one another and the wind died. Elena closed the door on them.

'You can't leave them out there,' Nicholas growled.

Elena shrugged. 'It's getting crowded in here.'

Andrews looked to his left. There was a long staff in an umbrella stand by the door. He grabbed it. 'I don't suppose . . .' He looked at his gun.

Nicholas shook his head. 'Not a chance.'

'Thought not.' He opened the door, stepped into the main room and closed it behind him. The noise swelled and quieted again as the door clicked shut.

I started to go after him.

'Wait!' It was Norah's voice again. 'We have to . . . stop this.'

'I know.' I lifted Matilda.

'No.' Norah licked her lips. 'There's only one way to . . . end this. You have to . . . shut the rift. If there's no magic—'

'There will be no zombies,' Olivia finished, nodding. 'They're

187

dead – so it's magic that's . . . keeping them moving. It has to be.'

Elena stepped closer to Norah. 'There's only one way,' she said, her voice mesmeric as she slinked nearer to the girls.

'No!' I limped swiftly after her. 'There's no way to bring your sister back, Norah! Look what happened to Isobel.'

'I'm casting . . . the spell.' Norah reached out and her hand closed over one of the blades lying beside her. My eyes were drawn towards Olivia, lying helplessly at her side.

'God, no. Norah, *please*!'

Nicholas stood frozen behind me looking from me to his sister, his mouth working as if he wanted to speak but had no idea what to say. He wanted Natalie back as much as she did.

Norah raised the knife. 'Consummavi,' she cried, her voice suddenly strong. 'Consummavi, *Consummavi*.' I hurled myself forward, trying to catch her wrist, but it was too late. With her eyes on Olivia's, Norah brought the knife down.

'Rise,' she croaked. 'Resurgemus . . .' She struck, the knife biting deep into her own stomach. Nicholas yelled as Norah sagged backwards.

'Resurgemus,' she gasped. '*Danny*!'

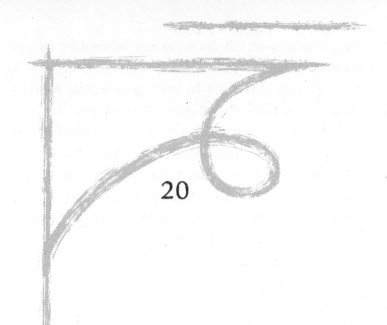

20

NOTHING HAPPENED. For a long moment, there was only Norah bleeding out on to the floor, the echo of her spell hanging in the air and the sounds of fighting from the room outside.

'Oh no, Norah! What did you do that for?' I hadn't seen Nicholas move but he was on his knees beside her, pulling the knife out as she twitched in pain.

She looked past him, her eyes meeting mine. 'I can't hear it . . . any more.'

'The hound? You've been hearing it all this time?' I held Matilda like a comforter.

'It was right . . . outside.' Norah lay very still – only her lips moved.

Elena leant into me. 'There's not enough life force left for it to draw on,' she whispered.

'Oh God.' Tears choked me. I'd failed again. Another teenager was dead because of me. And I'd promised to help her.

Nicholas threw the knife behind him and it clattered against the counter as he tore off his shirt. Rolling it into a ball, he held it against Norah's stomach. 'Please,' he was whispering. 'Please, please.' His bare back was bent, shadows spread over his skin.

Gran started to yowl piteously. Only Olivia was quiet, looking at Norah with horror in her gaze.

'I feel better,' Norah said, and she smiled a little . . . then she closed her eyes.

'Ivy?' I jerked around. Danny was standing in front of me, an unfamiliar look of confusion and fear on his face. 'Ivy?' He held out a hand, then collapsed.

I caught him before I'd even thought to move. I put my arms around his skinny ribcage and held him close to my chest. He *smelt* like Danny – Lynx deodorant, boy sweat and soap. His face was against my throat, his shaggy blonde hair tickled my ear. I tensed, half expecting those white teeth to start gnawing my throat. My skin tingled in fearful anticipation. Nothing happened.

'D—Danny?' I couldn't let him go. I held him like a gift I'd never thought to receive. I heard the rasp of his breathing – panting almost. His fingers clutched at me convulsively.

'Ivy?' He said again.

Elena drifted towards us like someone in a dream. 'It worked,' she said reaching out to touch his back and then his hair. 'He's alive.'

Gran sniffed his leg and then rubbed her face against his calf. Danny looked down. 'H—hello, Mrs Bolton.'

Nicholas looked up, shuddering with what I'd thought was grief but now realised was anger. 'How? You said that spell wouldn't work.'

'It wasn't *innocent blood* that was needed,' I said with sudden realisation. 'It was *sacrifice*. That's how you bring back the dead. A life for a life: given willingly for the one they want to bring back.' I tightened my arms around Danny. I didn't want to look at his face, part of me was still terrified that he would look like Violet had – madness in his eyes.

'A mistranslation,' Elena said with a little chuckle.

'You think this is *funny*?' Nicholas lurched to his feet.

Elena shook her head and I finally screwed up my courage. I pushed Danny to arm's length. 'Let me look at you.'

He half-ducked into that stoop I knew so well, staring at me through his heavy fringe.

'You look the same.' I found my gaze going to his throat. He was whole and well. 'I don't believe it.'

Elena stroked his back again. 'You're really here.'

He twisted to take her in. 'You've been bad, E.' He turned back to me. 'And you look older, Ivy. I like your T-shirt though.'

'I *am* older.' I let go of one of his arms and touched his face wonderingly. 'I missed you.'

'Well, I'm glad you're all happy,' Nicholas choked. He looked at his sister, her face had smoothed out and she was no longer in pain . . . or afraid. It was horrible.

Gran slunk over and licked Norah's hand, as if she expected the girl to start stroking her.

Olivia turned her face to the wall, but Nicholas bent down and slid his arms under her. Olivia's eyes widened and she squeaked in pain as he lifted her up, biceps straining. She curled into his shoulder and wrapped her arms around his neck.

'What are you doing?' I didn't dare move closer.

'Norah wanted you to close the rift – that's what her sacrifice was for. So, let's close the rift.'

Gran looked up. 'You can't take that girl out there!' She batted his leg.

I forced my eyes up to his tortured face. 'Gran's right.'

'You want to leave her here . . . defenceless?' Nicholas's gaze was fixed, as if he knew he'd crumple if he caught sight of his sister.

'I'm *sorry*, N—'

'Save it.' Nicholas started forwards.

'Wait just a minute. *Please*.' He hesitated, willing to listen at least, so I turned to Elena. 'Gather what you need to cast the original spell, just the way we did it the first time.' I dragged my hands through my ponytail, unconsciously neatening it. 'We're going to have to fight our way out.'

'Why are those things still out there?' Gran miaowed, leaving Norah and jumping on to the counter. 'I thought they were after *Isobel*.' She pointedly didn't look at the bloody jacket covering the body in the centre of the floor.

'They won't be compelled to keep coming any more,' Elena said, 'but there's food out there. That's what they're after now.' She grabbed a bag from behind the counter and shoved the *Necronomicon* inside before adding candles from a display, a copper bowl, scissors, a lighter, compass and matches.

'Food . . . you mean us?' I curled a lip. 'I hate you right now!'

'We'll still have to fight our way through. But if we can get past the zombies, we can get to the cemetery.' Elena slung the bag over her shoulder, reached behind the counter and pulled out a baseball bat. 'Then we can shut this thing down.'

I lifted my crutch in one hand and Matilda in the other. 'Danny, stay between us,' I said.

'But I—'

'Danny – we aren't losing you again. Plus, like you said, I'm older than you now so you have to listen to me. Stay with Nicholas and Olivia in the *middle*.' I limped to the door. 'Ready?'

No one answered so I opened the door anyway.

Immediately I was assaulted by noise – shrieking and wailing, yelling and the thunder of running feet. It seemed as if my vision was tinged red, but it was blood that had splashed over the room. The Chinese twins were still slumped, exhausted, against the wall beside me. Andrews stood in front of them, big as a tank, wielding his staff as if he'd been trained by a Nepalese monk in a hidden valley.

There were still groups of teens huddling against the back wall. Others had overturned tables and hid behind those. There was a small group hiding with the DJ in his booth. Many more fought with sticks and chair legs, in pairs or trios, trying to keep the zombies back.

At least the zombies moved with no co-ordination, unable to team up, just desperate to feed. For a moment I thought the kids were winning and my heart lifted – then I saw the purple-haired girl. She was face down on a table, her hands hanging limply on each side of the wooden top. As I watched her fingers started to twitch, and she raised her head. Like Isobel, she was dead, her eyes filmy . . . and she was hungry. She turned, and in a swift, jerky movement she leapt on to the back of a pimply boy holding a splintered railing. She sank her teeth into his neck. He screamed and dropped his weapon and I cried out as he plunged to the floor with the girl like a monkey on his back, still tearing at his skin.

Every fallen teen was going to rise again. We were going to lose.

'Where the hell are the police?' Nicholas grunted as I started forward, trying to look in all directions at once.

Andrews spotted us. 'Where are you going?'

'Help clear us a path and you'll find out,' I spat. A zombie in a dirty chef's apron lunged for my arm and I swung Matilda viciously. He took the blade in his shoulder but kept coming. I yanked Matilda free and staggered backwards. Elena leapt forward and smashed her bat into his face. This time he went to his knees. I swung the machete again – at his neck this time. Matilda stuck and Elena put her hands on mine to help me pull her free. Danny kicked the man backwards and he fell and stopped moving.

'Zombies, Ivy,' Danny yelled. 'You gotta go for the head.'

'I know! Stay *back*.' I spun again, seeking the next attack. The room was still lit by disco bulbs; the semi-darkness an added layer to the horror. Coloured lights strobed over the melee, highlighting moments of horror and unbelievable bravery.

The androgyne was standing back to back against a boy with huge shoulders wearing a vintage *Messi* football top. He was using a chair to push a fat zombie away from them both.

Three girls who had been cowering against the wall, suddenly jumped up. They had spotted a younger boy cornered by a dead woman in running gear. All three rushed her, swinging their bags and using the flashes on their phones to distract her long enough for the boy to roll to freedom.

The light blinked away from them. When it turned back on, the jogger had one of the girls by the hair. I looked quickly away.

There was a scream to my right and a blue light picked out a little boy wearing a dinosaur raincoat – he was savaging the leg of a gorgeous dark-skinned girl who fell, sobbing under his attack.

Behind me Olivia was crying, Elena was gasping harshly and Nicholas was panting with effort as we pushed forward. To my right I heard the thud and smack of Andrews' staff as he fought to clear a path to us.

Movement in my periphery. I whirled – a man in a blue uniform was coming for me. For a second I hesitated to lift Matilda, thinking help had arrived, but then I realised the man's teeth were bared and bloody. I reeled backwards, trying to bring Matilda up, yet knowing it was too late. A shot rang out. The sound beat into my ears like a hand clap and the man fell sideways with a crimson hole in his forehead. Eyes wide, I pushed on silently thanking Nicholas.

The doorway was in front of us, a short run away. There was a cluster of teens between us and it, but it was almost clear. All the zombies who could, had entered the building.

'The door!' I yelled as loudly as I could. 'Everyone – out of the building!'

The teenagers nearest us looked up, then towards the doorway. There was a shout and a wave of movement.

I let the crowd take us. I still held Matilda and so I lifted her to head height, trying not to hurt anyone and looking wildly around to make sure that Danny remained with me. 'Grab my crutch.' I thrust it at him, and he understood, holding on to the rubber bung at the end. It took me a little off balance, but I could still hobble.

'Where's Gran?' I yelled. Nicholas tapped my shoulder and pointed. I looked to see Gran clinging on to Elena's bag, claws dug into the canvas and a grim expression on her feline face. Her tail stood directly up behind her, fat as a bottle brush. I'd have laughed, but it wasn't really funny.

There was a scream next to me and a kid fell with a zombie on top of him. I sliced Matilda into the creature's back, hoping it wasn't too late. And then we were climbing the stairs and heading through the broken doorway.

The kill box was right in front of us, the broken door open to the dark alley and a lamp-lit London night. The zombie trapped by the ankle remained, jerking, in the entrance. I tried to hold back, but the pressure of the terrified crowd drove me on, my feet barely touching the ground. 'Elena!' I yelled.

'*Incensa.*' Her voice came from behind me and I ducked as fire spurted ahead of us and incinerated the thing where it stood.

We tumbled past the burning zombie into the open air – among the throng of sobbing, shrieking kids.

There were flashing lights at the end of the lane. 'Finally,' Nicholas snarled. 'What are they waiting for?'

I figured that either they hadn't been able to – or hadn't *wanted* to – get past the zombie that had been trapped in the doorway.

I pulled Danny sideways against the bins and sheathed Matilda. Elena followed. 'We don't have time to speak to the police. Let the kids distract them.'

We allowed twenty or thirty teenagers and the DJ, who was half-carrying an injured boy, to stumble past. Then Andrews backed out of the building, holding a pair of zombies back with his staff. The Chinese twins cowered in his shadow.

As soon as the duo reached the open air, he propelled them to the left of the exit with a kick, slammed the broken door shut with his staff and leant heavily against it. Half of me wanted to help him hold the door closed, the other half wondered how many kids he was trapping inside. Had he, like his 'numbers people', calculated the 'collateral damage'?

I shuddered and hustled Danny and Elena towards the alley's end, steadfastly ignoring the sound of splintering wood behind us.

'Hey, you!' A burly policeman strode in our direction, looking at Nicholas. 'Did *you* make the call? What exactly is happening?'

'We have to get to the cemetery, ignore him.' I turned to Nicholas, but he was staggering away from us. Meeting the policeman, he thrust Olivia into his arms. The man grunted under her weight.

'Gunshot wound to the stomach,' Nicholas snapped, his voice clear even over the shouting and sobbing that surrounded us. 'She needs to get to a hospital.' The policeman's eyes widened and I saw Nicholas say something more quietly and point back towards the building. Norah.

The policeman started to speak, but Nicholas shook his head. Then I heard Andrews' dismayed groan and I spun to see the wooden door splinter apart. Fragments flew and Andrews sailed back, landing awkwardly on his spine as the first zombies appeared. Three of them jumped him as he held his staff desperately up, like the bar of a fairground ride. Others scampered straight past, chasing the escaping kids. Police reached for their radios and one fired his weapon.

'Aim for their heads!' I yelled. It was all I could do. I continued to push Danny ahead of me, past the police cars and ambulances.

I dodged a paramedic, who tried to get me to stop, and limped into the street. Elena was on my tail and the paramedic yelped as she found out just how much Elena didn't want to be examined. Then we were racing towards the cemetery entrance – Gran bouncing on Elena's shoulder, Danny's long legs allowing him to pull ahead.

I hated leaving the police and remaining kids. Who knew how many were still in the building; too injured, scared or trapped to run? I itched to take Matilda and return to save as many as I could. But we had a chance to shut this down before it spread further, and I had to take it.

Someone gripped my elbow to hurry me and I looked up. Nicholas was at my side, his face forbiddingly grim. 'Are you all right?' I gasped.

He shook his head. His sister's blood was embedded in his nails, Olivia's smeared his chest and his hair was standing on end. He looked primal, but his eyes were haunted. He definitely wasn't all right. His leather shoes made a clipped sound on the pavement – a businessman from the waist down. Half wild. I didn't know what to say to him.

'Miss Mann, *stop!*' It was Andrews.

I kept my head down and my pace up. My ponytail bounced on my shoulders, oddly peppy. Lurching from streetlight to streetlight, we raced – knowing that every second we left that rift open was a second another kid could die.

'Don't stop!' Nicholas said.

'Not going to!' We were at the ivy-covered wall. Danny was already vanishing into the curtain of greenery. It swung behind him, leached of colour by the deepening night. Elena was on his tail.

Running footsteps behind us. '*Stop right there!*'

I turned my head but let Nicholas keep pulling me on. 'It's Andrews,' I gasped. 'He won't let us do this.'

'*He won't have a choice!*' We reached the doorway and Nicholas shunted me through like a kid.

'Come on.' I reached back for his hand, but he shook his head and pulled the gun from the belt of his trousers.

'I'll hold him off.'

I hesitated and then nodded. In a straight fight I'd have bet on Andrews, but Nicholas had the advantage, or rather, he had the gun ... and we only needed a bit of time. Andrews would have nothing to fight for if we could make the spell work.

'Be careful.' It was a stupid thing to say but Nicholas nodded anyway and I turned and left him.

21

THE CEMETERY WAS dark and quiet. Somewhere an owl hooted and a fox yipped in apparent reply – clear even over the faint growling that still rumbled in my ears. The sounds of London at night were oddly muffled as if the high wall was somehow soundproof. I heard distant sirens mixed with yelling and the cries of the injured, but it all seemed far away. I stumbled from grave to grave. This time I turned left, towards Violet's, knowing it was where I would find Elena and Danny.

'This way,' I said, looking down. Gran had waited for me.

'I know the way.' I hobbled beside her, my leg aching like blazes, and she pressed her furry body against my shin, almost tripping me. I didn't need the added challenge in keeping my balance, but I let her do it. She said nothing, but she was the picture of a freaked-out feline: her tail remained stiffer than a pine, the fur on her back formed a mohawk and she was hissing like a snapped electric cable.

The crack of gunfire shivered through my bones and I stiffened, then kept walking. I had to trust that Nicholas would be fine.

'Ivy,' Gran said eventually. 'I'm worried about you.'

I looked down and forced a smile. 'I'll be fine.'

Gran ignored me. 'I'm worried because you just . . . cut that girl's head off.'

I stopped walking and stared. 'She was a zombie, Gran. She'd have killed us all.'

'Yes,' Gran said and she sat down, her tail waving erratically . . . nervously. 'And I'm glad you stopped her. It's just . . . everyone else hesitated, but not you. It was . . . too easy for you to do that.'

I exhaled and staggered back to lean on a crumbling gravestone. 'You're saying you think I'm . . . a psycho?'

Gran miaowed anxiously.

'I'm not,' I yelled at her. 'I was doing my *job*. Protecting people means making hard choices. You'd rather I waited, let her turn Andrews and then have to deal with both of them?'

'That's not what I—'

'You're not being fair,' I shouted, stamping my crutch against hard earth. 'You're just like everyone else – blaming me. I made *one* mistake.' I gasped and my vision blurred. 'It wasn't as if I set out to mess up the world! I watched my dead best friend kill my boyfriend. But no one told me it was OK. *No one* was on my side.' I lurched upright. 'I was kicked out of school, Gran! I lost all of my friends. Mum *left*, Dad followed as soon as he could. The government treated me like a lab rat for *two years*. I'm on my own, so I have to make up my own rules. Everyone leaves me and

I'm *still* expected to make the right decision every time. Do the compassionate thing. Be the adult. Well as far as I can tell, being an adult means blaming and *leaving people*. So I've got harder, it just makes it easier to be *me*. I'm not some maniac! Why is it OK for me to protect everyone else, and not myself?'

Gran stared at me. 'Ivy . . . I'm sorry.'

'*You're* sorry.' I spun around. 'I'm sorry, everyone's sorry, but they always want someone to blame. And that's me, isn't it? It's always *me*.'

'I wasn't blaming you.' Gran approached me, her tail weaving from side to side, her eyes wide, her whiskers twitching. 'I hadn't realised what this life had made you. I hadn't seen it before.'

'And what has it made me?' I leant down to her.

'Hard,' Gran said sadly. 'It's made you hard and . . . lonely.' She butted her head against my leg. 'I'm not blaming you. I'm blaming Beverley.'

'Bev—?'

'Your mum.'

'I know who B—'

'She should never have left you. Who does that?'

'Lots of people do, Gran.' I straightened.

'I thought I'd raised her better.' She nudged me again. 'So, I suppose I'm to blame. For raising a quitter and . . .' She hesitated and looked up at me. 'And when you brought me back I felt like I had a new chance at life, a chance to have all the fun I missed but what I should have been doing was looking after *you*. Looking after my family.' Her tail finally stopped waving. 'I'm not your pet, Ivy,' she mewed softly. 'I'm your grandmother and I'm so sorry you've felt so alone.'

I froze. 'You're . . . apologising to me?'

She butted my leg again and I leant down to stroke her. 'When the rift's shut I won't need to do this job any more.'

'That's good,' Gran said. She looked behind her. 'We'd better get that done then.'

I nodded and turned towards Vi's open grave.

'So . . .' she said after a few steps. 'Danny.'

'You said you'd seen him. You were right.' I skirted a low marble memorial, its letters sunken in the moonlight.

'What will you do about him? Will you tell his parents?'

'I haven't even thought about it.'

'Is he going to live with *us*?' Gran glowered. 'It's a small flat.'

'I haven't—'

'I'm just saying—'

'*Gran!*' A dog barked and Gran stiffened. 'It's only a dog,' I said.

'One of them devil dogs?' Gran looked around wildly. 'Of course, they're all devil dogs,' she muttered. I bent down and finally picked her up, stroking her tawny head with my fingertips.

'Better?'

She hissed at me but snuggled in firmly. 'I know I'm meant to be looking after *you* now, but . . . don't put me down.'

I kept going, hugging Gran's warm body to my chest. Her claws dug into my bra, but I didn't try and shift her. There were lights straight ahead – flickering candles. A grave that had never been filled back in, sharp lettering on marble: *Violet Dawn Adams*. I held Gran more tightly. 'We're here.'

Things had changed, at least a little. There was a range of monitoring equipment aimed at the centre of the grave, beeping steadily and quietly. The grave itself had been dug out neatly – a rectangle left open to the sky, rather than the ragged hole that Vi had created when she rose. Her splintered coffin was missing.

I knew the rift was right there, spilling dark matter into the world, but there was nothing to see. No shimmer in the air, no rip in the fabric of reality . . . just that gentle, steady beeping.

'Will this work without Violet?' I asked shakily, looking at Elena and digging my fingers more deeply into Gran's fur.

Elena nodded. 'I've been researching this almost since it happened. I believe the rift was torn open by the words we used – our syllables and actions, the time and place. It was a kind of side effect of what we were doing. So, it wasn't specifically Violet's rising that . . .' She tailed off. 'I'm not sure I'm making sense.'

'I get it. The Commission's research team thought the same thing a couple of years ago. We can't do a spell reversal, like we did on the floor, because we didn't cast a spell meant to open the rift. It's more like . . . we opened a door and now we need to do the same thing to close it. The same words and actions in the same place, at the same time.'

'Yes. Danny's always been the missing ingredient.'

'I'm not an *ingredient*.' He was staring at the ground to the right of my feet and I realised that it was the place he'd died. I put Gran down and took his hand instead.

Elena brushed her hands through her spiky hair, inhaled deeply and laid the *Necronomicon* in front of Vi's gravestone.

'I hate that book.' Every page seemed stained with something unspeakable and creased and greasy, as if made with something other than simple paper. The light of the candle beside the headstone licked the underside of the cover, turning it red.

Elena ignored me. 'Danny's laid the candles out already.'

'I can see that.' I squeezed his hand. 'Are you all right?'

'It's weird being here. I'm trying not to think about it.' He forced his eyes away from the patch of ground that still seemed soaked with his blood. 'Maybe we can get a McDonalds after?'

'Sure. I'll buy.'

'Well, *I* haven't got any money.' He shuffled his feet and offered a small smile.

Elena pulled four small glasses and a sports bottle from her bag. 'We had Evian last time,' I commented, leaning closer.

'That shouldn't matter.' She filled each glass and put one at the base of each candle. The flames reflected in the glimmering liquid, trapped stars.

I looked up. '*Is* it the right time?' There were clouds over the moon, which hung bulbous above us.

Elena nodded. 'As near as I can tell.' She handed me the pair of scissors and held the copper bowl up. 'I need some hair.'

'I remember.' I sliced a chunk from my ponytail without even looking, then I cut Danny's for him. I reached over and snipped an unnecessarily large chunk from Elena's, right above her left eyebrow. Let her try and find a hairdresser fancy enough to fix *that*. I dropped all the hair into the bowl where it fluttered in the night wind, strands blowing away over the grass.

Elena burned the remaining hair, releasing the stink into the night. Then I realised that the only way to put the bowl between the candles was to sit it inside Vi's open grave. Elena saw the same thing. She swayed as if she was going to faint.

'It's OK,' I reached for the bowl. 'I'll do it.'

Elena hesitated. 'Sorry.' She looked at my hand. 'I'll pass the bowl down to you.'

'All right.' I climbed awkwardly into the pit, jamming my toecaps into the sheer wall and blackening my hands on the loose earth. I dangled and then jumped the last couple of feet. Immediately the world shrank to the rectangle of stars directly above my head, and the looming edges of Vi's headstone. They'd dug the hole deep.

I reached up. Elena had to lie on the ground and stretch to pass the vessel down. I took it, careful not to spill the burned offering.

'I guess we'll get started on the circle,' I heard Danny say. I pictured him kneeling in the darkness and humping damp mud between his palms, his knees in the dirt. I hoped Elena was helping and that it was impossible to get grave dirt out of leather grain.

I laid the stinking dish carefully in the centre of the hole, sinking it slightly into the moist soil to make sure I couldn't accidentally kick it over when I was pulled out. My injured thigh ached and bled into the earth. I hoped that wouldn't change things.

Suddenly I heard a voice shouting and the pounding of heavy feet on loam. 'Stop what you're doing!'

'It's Andrews!' I reached up. 'Get me out.' But no one appeared to help me.

I dug my toes into the pit's edge but succeeded only in bringing down a scattering of dirt. I was stuck until someone reached down for me.

'You're too late!' Elena's voice.

'This isn't what we agreed, Miss Monroe.' I heard Andrews stop at the graveside.

'Where's Nicholas?' Danny's voice was higher-pitched, afraid.

'He'll be fine.' I sagged in relief as I heard Andrews' reply. 'But

I do have my gun back, so if you would be kind enough to move *away* from the rift site.'

'We can't do that.' Elena's shadow moved as she sidled closer to Andrews and I dug my nails into my palms. If Andrews shot her, we'd be screwed. He had to know that.

'You saw what happened tonight,' Danny cried. 'You can't want things like that to keep happening.'

'Boy, you'd still be dead if we didn't have magic,' Andrews said. 'Why would you want to get rid of it?'

There was a smack of flesh on flesh, Danny grunted and I wondered what Andrews had done to him. I tried again to climb out of the grave – roots were sticking out of the dirt and I tried pulling on them, only to give myself another shower of grit.

Suddenly Gran dropped into the hole and I almost screamed.

'Stay down!' She hissed and dug her claws into my leg, forcing me into a crouch. 'I don't think he knows you're in here and you don't want to be up there right now.'

I swept her into my arms and looked skywards. The stars blinked coldly down at me. It didn't *feel* as if I was standing in the centre of a magical rift with dark matter saturating my body. But, I shuddered, I *did* feel as if I was standing in the now-empty grave of my best friend, where she had laid for a year rotting. I *really* wanted to get out. The dog howled in the distance and the snarling in my ears seemed to intensify in reply. I shivered. Danny was standing up to a maniac with a gun. If Andrews killed him, no questions would be asked. Who would miss a dead boy?

There was nothing I could do, no way I could protect him. I was helpless.

I stared upwards, burning a hole in the sky and wishing I could see what was going on. The dog barked again – my ears tingled, and I froze.

It was possible that I did have a single play left. It was also possible that it wouldn't work, or that I'd be dragged off to hell. But then, no one had ever survived a hound's attack before. So maybe I'd been on borrowed time since the first day I met Norah Ortega.

'Gran . . .?'

She looked up at me, huge pupils making her green eyes luminous.

'If I lift you up,' I whispered. 'Do you think you can knock the *Necronomicon* down here without being seen?'

Gran stared at me, saying nothing. Her whiskers twitched. Finally, she batted my face with a paw. 'Are you planning something that is going to get you killed, Ivy Elizabeth?'

I stroked her flank. 'I hope not,' I said.

'Fine then.' Gran turned her head to face the side of the grave. 'Lift me up.'

I boosted Gran as high as I could, very glad that she hadn't asked for details, and she scrabbled the rest of the way out. Her tail waved as it vanished and I edged to the rear of the pit and pressed my back against the dirt.

'Put that down,' Andrews was saying. 'Right now!' I didn't know what he was talking about, but at least he was distracted. Knowing Danny, he'd be trying something heroic. 'Just wait for me, Danny,' I prayed. 'Just wait.'

A thud. The *Necronomicon* landed at my feet in a shower of filth. I strained to hear Andrews, but he didn't mention the book or Gran.

Well done, Gran.

I picked the book up. I knew what I was going to do. I'd been hearing a hell hound for the last couple of weeks and now I was going to try to set it on Andrews and hope I could stop it before it killed the rest of us. It was probably suicide.

I flicked quietly through the faintly tacky pages, each stuck slightly to my fingertips as though desperate to be read. How would I know which page? It had been a long time since I'd studied the book. I stopped, my hand trembling. A photograph had been jammed inside one of the pages . . . a bookmark. I lifted it up to the moonlight and saw Norah, Nicholas and their little sister, Natalie. Nicholas had his arm around both sisters – his hair was longer than I was used to and a little messy and he was grinning widely. Natalie was sticking her tongue out and Norah was rolling her eyes.

Perhaps Norah had put it there to remind her why she was doing the spell, to stop herself from backing out. Tears pricked my eyes.

I had maybe moments before Andrews worked out where I was. I had none of the ingredients Norah would have used and I could hardly see the lettering on the page. But what I did have was an apparent connection to a monster. Its saliva was in my blood, infectious as the zombie pathogen. It was definitely doing something to me – forging a connection perhaps. Eating away at my soul? Possibly.

I put the book on the floor, took the lighter out of my vest and flicked it on. I held it close to the page, hoping the glow wouldn't give me away.

'Where is she?' Andrews' voice. 'There were three of you. You wouldn't be here without the insufferable Miss Mann.' *Prick.*

'She went back.' Danny replied. 'She said she'd rejoin us when we had the spell set up. She wanted to make sure the kids at the club were all safe.'

'And she wanted to check on Olivia,' Elena added.

Clever. That was believable.

I read the spell and sighed quietly. This was going to hurt. Wincing, I used Matilda to slice a long cut in my left arm and let the blood drip between my feet.

I'd have to skip most of the incantation but I was literally standing in the centre of a magical rift and if I could hear the hound, I had to believe it could hear me.

This had to work.

'*Aperire portal*,' I whispered. Open the portal. I thought briefly about how hard I'd worked to close it and now I was magicking the thing back open. '*Canis venerunt.*' Hound, come!

I felt a familiar tugging in my chest and my blood ran more freely as if a tap had been turned on. That was worrying. The growling tinnitus in my ears paused and then changed to a howl.

'*Aperire portal, canis venerunt.*'

'What was that?' Andrews voice. His head suddenly appeared above the open grave and he grinned. 'What are you *doing*, Miss Mann?' He pointed his gun at me. The slick muzzle shone with reflections of candle flames.

I looked up at him. '*Aperire portal, canis venerunt!*' I shouted the last and blood gushed from my leg and arm, making me dizzy. It felt as if my heart was being dragged towards the wound. I thought desperately about Andrews, hoping that would be enough to set the hound hunting him first.

Then the growl moved from inside my head and reverberated

210

around the cemetery. The sound took hold of the base of my spine and gnawed at the marrow. I collapsed to my knees.

Elena screamed.

Andrews spun around and I heard the sharp retort of gunfire. Gran skidded down the open graveside, looking as if she'd been electrocuted. 'Ivy, you *have* to be kidding!' She screamed.

I ignored her. 'Danny, get down here!' I shouted.

I'd barely finished speaking when he rolled into the grave, landing on top of me with his arms and legs swinging.

'What *is* that?' He had blood on his face, and I could see the whites of his eyes. 'What if it jumps down here? We'll be shredded.'

Elena shrieked again and the gun fired once more. I yanked the bell, Bible and flare out of my vest. 'I'm going to exorcise it.' I held my equipment in trembling hands. 'Elena, don't you get killed!'

There was a roar and something that felt like warm rain spattered my upturned face.

'Oh God,' Danny stared at me.

'*Elena!*' I screamed.

It was her turn to roll into Violet's grave. Danny caught her. She was holding her left arm. Arms were not meant to twist in that direction. Her face was covered in blood and she was panting. 'It's getting crowded in here,' Gran wailed.

I shook Elena's good shoulder. 'Andrews?'

'Dead . . .' Elena swallowed. 'I mean . . . no one could survive that.'

I realised the sound I could hear was teeth tearing into flesh. A dog gnawing at a bone. Tears were running down my face. I'd killed a man.

Suddenly the sounds ceased, and a low growl restarted.

I looked at Elena, she was slumped against the wall of the pit looking as if she was using the last of her energy to remain on her feet. I looked at Danny. I really didn't want to ask him to do this.

'Danny,' I whispered.

'Yes?' He didn't take his eyes from the rectangle of starts above us.

'I'm going to need you to take Matilda.' I handed him the machete as he blinked. 'When the hound sticks its head over the edge of the pit, all I need you to do is cut it.'

'Cut it . . . right.' He sounded unsure.

'The thing is fed now – it's got both feet on the mortal plane. Only a full exorcism is going to get rid of it, so I need its blood to banish it.'

Elena raised her head. 'What can I do?'

'Just give Danny a boost.' I set my feet either side of the bowl. I was feeling pretty faint myself – my arm and leg still bled freely, and I was shaky and light-headed with hunger as if I'd burned through my fuel reserves in a single massive bonfire. Nausea twisted in my empty stomach.

I just had to hold on a bit longer. I thought of my bed and it was the most vivid fantasy I'd ever had.

Gran smacked my ankle. 'Stay with us, Ivy.'

I shook myself and gripped the bell tightly. I took a deep breath and rang the bell. The sound jingled out of the pit and into sky.

The hound's massive head appeared, blocking out the stars. It started to roar and then it stopped, looking at me with its head cocked to one side. It whined like a puppy, its eyes burning into mine. Did it remember me? Could it sense our connection?

'What are you waiting for?' Gran yowled.

'*Now*, Danny,' I cried.

Elena knelt on one knee and Danny leapt from her other one, slashing frantically upwards. The hound yelped and jumped back, but not before its blood splashed me. I felt horribly as if I'd betrayed it somehow.

'Well done, Danny!' I lit the little flare with my thumb and kicked the Bible open on top of the *Necronomicon*.

'*In the name of God the All-powerful, Father, Son, and Holy Ghost, of the Blessed Peter, Prince of the Apostles, and of all the saints, in virtue of the power which has been given us of binding and loosing in Heaven and on Earth,*' I inhaled quickly. '*I exclude you from the bosom of Earth, declare you anathematized and judge you condemned to eternal fire. I deliver you to Satan.*'

I rang the bell again and dropped the flare into the mud. The hound howled.

I slammed the Bible shut.

The sound was instantly cut off, switching once more from the air of the cemetery to an agonised wail that I still heard as a faint ringing in the back of my ears.

I stood, swaying and wheezing.

'I can't believe you did that,' Elena gasped.

I had to take a couple of tries to get my equipment back in my vest. Danny handed Matilda back to me with a trembling hand.

'Well done, Ivy.' Gran's eyes glowed. 'But you can't rest yet. There's still a zombie problem. How are we going to get out of here?'

I examined the crumbling wall of the pit and groaned.

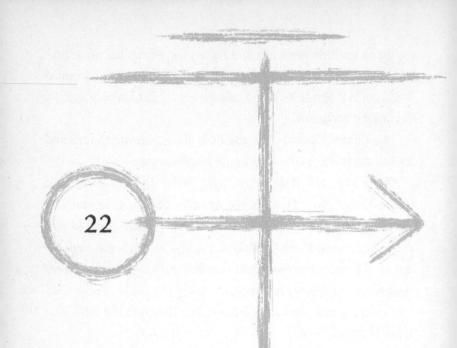

22

DANNY WAS TRYING to lift me on to his shoulders when Nicholas turned up. 'Ivy?'

'In here,' Danny replied for me.

His head appeared. 'What are you doing? And where's Andre—' His voice petered out. 'Oh . . .'

I didn't want to know what he'd seen. I could guess.

'Can you get us out?' Gran snapped.

Nicholas reached down and his palm slapped into mine. Wishing I'd done a few more sit-ups in my time I scrambled at the pit walls, sprinkling Elena with grit, until my chest dragged on the grass. That put my eyes level with what was left of Andrews. There wasn't much. I gagged, spun and reached down for Danny.

Elena tossed Gran up, then she tucked the *Necronomicon* into her belt and allowed Nicholas to pull her free as she held her broken arm to her chest.

'That was . . . intense.' She pulled the book out, glanced at Andrews and then away. 'But it's nearly over.'

'I hope so.' Without thinking I leant against Nicholas, who paused and then put an arm around me. I glanced in the direction of Emporium, then I stiffened. 'Oh . . . please, no!'

The things coming towards us moved like stop-motion photography – where they *seemed* slow and jerky, but suddenly were closer. I heard moans and growls, inhuman noises. Among the group, the moonlight picked out short skirts and glow stick necklaces. The kids who hadn't made it.

I so desperately wanted to be wrong. 'Nicholas . . . is that . . .?'

He dropped his arm, as if he'd been shot. 'Zombies.'

'This is the most direct route from Emporium back to central London,' Elena grimaced. 'The fastest way to the most concentrated food source.'

'Plus, they can probably smell Andrews' blood.' I tried not to point at the corpse desecrating Violet's gravesite. I was light-headed with horror and exhaustion. 'What is it with this day?'

'Cast the spell,' Danny said. 'Quickly.'

I nodded and took a deep breath. 'Nicholas, you'd better back away. It was just the three of us first time and I don't know how you'd effect . . .' He was already moving, retreating among the gravestones until he was nothing but a shadowy figure. I looked again at the zombies. They were closer. Much closer. I could make out their injuries, but not the whites of their eyes. We had time. I hoped. I turned to Elena. 'Let's do this.'

Elena looked at the book. *'From cloud to sea.'*

Danny and I repeated after her, just as we had the first time. I caught his hand and squeezed it. He looked at me, our eyes level this time. He still had so much growing to do.

'*From crown to throne. From blood to bough, from skin to bone.*'

The words returned to my tongue as though they'd always been there, waiting. I swayed and Danny shifted so that his arm was around me, holding me up. My body ached appallingly, and my leg throbbed like it was infected. Plus I'd lost my crutch.

Elena's face was deathly white under the stars. I remembered the first time we'd been here – the faint shimmer in the air, the clear skies. I looked up. There were clouds scudding towards the moon.

'*From tree to root, from earth to sky, come now, make her death a lie.*'

Our voices were a harmony, lifting above the groans of the rushing zombies. I couldn't speak faster, couldn't rush. The words came as they willed.

'*For thou who sleeps in stone and clay, heed our call and rise this day. Enter through the mortal door, assemble flesh and walk once more. Quondam multo ambulant!*'

Suddenly the wind rose, twisting my ponytail and slapping it over my face and Danny's.

'*Quondam multo ambulant!*'

I dug my fingers into Danny's forearm and he clutched me tightly. I closed my eyes.

'*Quondam multo ambulant!*'

I groaned as it felt like my chest ripped open. I reached numb fingers to touch but I wasn't bleeding, at least not physically. Still, I could feel my life rushing away – decade by decade in a swollen

216

river. Elena collapsed. Danny tried to hold us both up, but I took him to the floor in a heap.

I looked past Violet's grave – the zombies were still coming, hands like claws, mouths open, saliva dripping wetly . . . they smelt food. I shifted my gaze, the monitor was still beeping, a steady, horrible metronome.

'Why isn't it working?' Elena gasped; she was holding her chest too.

'I don't know. You must have been wrong.' I rolled on to my back, too exhausted to even *try* and lift Matilda. I hoped the end came more quickly and cleanly than I imagined it would.

'Ivy!' Nicholas was yelling my name.

'Stay back,' I waved at him weakly. He kept coming, the shadow resolving into his face and body. 'You can't help us, Nicholas.' He paused. 'It didn't work. Run!' I choked on the last word. Nicholas didn't run, but he didn't come any closer either.

'We did everything the same,' Elena sobbed. 'Everything! Danny's *here*. It should have worked.' She pulled herself to a sitting position against Vi's grave and traced the outline of her name with a shaking finger. 'I was so *sure*.'

Danny stiffened against me. 'Not everything's the same,' he said quietly.

'It is! I didn't forget a thing.' Elena closed her eyes.

'The revenant,' Danny said. 'There's no Violet.'

'Elena said we wouldn't . . . need Vi.' I was almost too tired to lift my head now. Even my fingers were too weak to twitch. The rift was sucking me dry.

'She was wrong.' Danny pushed me gently to one side and detangled his legs from mine.

'What are you ... doing?' I tried to roll back to him.

He stood on trembling legs. 'One more thing happened that night.'

'What?' But I already knew the answer, it sank like a dagger of ice into my brain. I knew what the stupid, brave, heroic sixteen-year-old was going to do. 'Danny, please. No! I can't ...'

He bent and squeezed my fingers. 'If I can, you can! I love you, Ivy.'

'I love you too. Please Danny, don't.'

Elena opened her eyes. She looked at me, saying nothing.

'You bitch.' I sobbed. 'Tell him. Stop him.'

'I can't,' she whispered. 'I think he's right.'

'He's not. What if—' Danny was already walking away from me. He only had to go a few steps. He spread his arms.

I recognised her. The girl had once had purple hair but now it was matted with blood. Her sparkly blue dress was torn, and her tights were laddered. She had lost one shoe, but she moved like a skater. She tore Danny's throat out before I could say another word.

I screamed. But not wordlessly. I cast the first spell that came to mind. One I'd never forgotten. '*Animum suam! Animum suam! Animum suam!*'

Save his soul. It was a prayer and a wish and a desperate attempt to do something ... anything.

Danny's blood splashed my face and arced into Violet's grave. Into the rift. And everything just ... stopped.

Thuds as bodies slumped to the ground like falling fruit. Danny landed in a heap, graceless in death once again. His blank eyes stared into mine. The flow of energy from my chest cut abruptly off, like a fuse had blown in a socket. And, over it all, the single high-pitched beep of a machine with nothing more to count.

I screamed until I was hoarse. Until Nicholas raced to my side and wrapped his arms around me. Then I sobbed and shook in his arms. I buried my face in his chest and felt his heart against my cheek. Danny was dead. Again. I felt Nicholas's tears in my hair. Of course, his sister was dead too.

A furry body wrapped itself around my neck. 'Ivy.' It was Gran. She licked my cheek with a sandpaper tongue. 'Ivy . . .'

I blinked at her and managed to move my hand. 'You're still . . .'

'Still here.' Gran swallowed. 'Magic put my soul *in* the damned cat, but it's not what's keeping me alive.'

I nodded. Relieved. Elena had said Gran didn't need magic any more and it looked as if she was right. A dog barked again. 'That bloody dog,' said Gran looking up sharply. 'I'm going to claw its nose off.'

23

THE DOG KEPT barking, the sound drawing nearer. I tore my eyes from Danny's in time to see a whippet-like shape twisting between the gravestones, twisting towards us.

'A stray—' Nicholas started.

The high-pitched yipping drilled into my brain and Gran stiffened, claws like pins digging into my collarbone. '*I'll* deal with this,' she climbed off me.

'I—I—I . . .' the dog seemed to be barking. 'I—ee—I—ee—I—eeee.'

Gran stood beside me and hissed. The dog skidded to a halt, mud spraying into my mouth. 'I . . . eee,' it tilted its head to one side.

'Get out of here, you mutt.' Gran stalked forward, she swiped one claw towards the poor thing, and it skittered backwards, yelping.

'I—eee.' It skidded forward again on its front paws, as if it wanted to play with Gran. Then it looked up at me with its head tilted. It was a skinny thing – its ears and muzzle pointed. It was too dark to tell its actual colour, but there were patches of lighter – almost white – fur on the flank and legs, almost as if it was wearing socks. And it was definitely a boy.

'I—eee,'

'Hey, boy.' Tiredly, I reached out a hand.

Gran exploded into action but I caught her by the tail. She whipped round furiously and I dropped her quickly. 'Gran . . . wait a minute. Do you hear what I hear?'

'I—ee.' The dog barked.

'Is it . . .?' I leant closer.

'Probably has *rabies*,' Gran snapped.

'I—ee.' The dog looked at Gran and panted. 'Ms . . . Olton.'

'Oh my God.' I squirmed free of Nicholas and crawled towards the dog. '*Danny?*'

'I—ee.' Danny's tongue lolled. 'I—' he paused and pulled his tongue back into his mouth. 'I . . . vy.'

Elena gasped. 'How?'

'The spell.' I said, holding my fingers out. Danny came to sniff them. Gran batted at his nose and he scuttled backwards. 'It's the one I used on Gran. I didn't really think . . .'

'The dog was in the cemetery.' Elena said, coming nearer. 'You trapped Danny's soul in a *dog*.'

'A whippet, I think,' Nicholas said. He held his hand out too. 'Hi Danny.'

'Ich-las.' Danny barked happily.

Gran glowered up at me balefully. 'If you think he's coming home with us . . .'

* * *

Nicholas's car remained outside the cemetery where Andrews had parked it. The roof had caved in, but the engine worked. Nicholas had found the keys on what remained of Andrews. He helped me into the back. I looked at Elena.

'What will you do?'

'Vanish.' Elena looked at the bag over her shoulder. 'I made a deal with some very dangerous people. They'll know by now what happened. They'll have had cameras all over the cemetery.' Sirens wailed, screaming closer. 'They'll be waiting for the police to clear.' She looked towards Emporium, 'I reckon I've got about half an hour.'

'You've got a plan?' Nicholas asked.

Elena nodded and I was pleased to see her hair looked *awful*. She held her injured arm carefully at her side. 'I've always got a plan.'

'And you're so good at running away.' I stared at my boots, so crusted with blood and filth they were misshapen. 'A lot of people died because of you.' I looked back up at her.

She sighed. 'I know. And a lot of people have died over the years because of what we did. But no more.'

I nodded. Gran put a paw on my leg. Danny whined.

'I can still hear the hound,' I said wryly, pointing to my ears.

Elena stared. 'That's not possible, not without magic.'

I shrugged. 'Then the connection's not magical. Its saliva infected me, I guess I'm stuck with it.'

Elena nodded.

'Will I ever see you again?'

'I doubt it.' She started to hobble away. 'It's not in the plan.'

'Right.' I watched her getting smaller, disappearing into the darkness. 'Bye, Elena.'

She didn't turn around. 'Bye, Ivy!'

✳ ✳ ✳

I let Danny and Gran into the flat and leant on the wall. Nicholas had half-carried me up the stairs. 'I'm *so* sorry,' I said as I undid my flack vest. 'I wanted to save Norah. I *tried*.'

Nicholas's face went carefully blank.

'I know you blame me.' I threw Matilda towards the hall table. I missed and she landed on the floor, sticking into a floorboard. There went the deposit. 'It's my fault.'

There was a yowl from inside the flat. 'Not on the sofa, you dumb *dog*!' Gran screeched.

I sighed. 'I wish . . .'

'I know.' Nicholas traced my chin with a finger. He stepped closer and instinctively I pressed back against the wall. I came up to his shoulder and was forced to tilt my head upwards to keep looking at him.

I blushed.

His phone rang and he pulled it out of his pocket, glanced at the screen and then retreated – turning his back on me. I frowned and laid my palms on the wall as he put the phone to his ear. The paintwork was cold and very real, very solid. If it wasn't for my freakish tinnitus, I could almost imagine the whole day had been a dream. The empty vodka glass was on the sideboard. Maybe I was still drunk. I *felt* drunk.

I tried not to listen to Nicholas's conversation – I'd have gone deeper into the flat, but my legs were like jelly. The only way I was getting to bed was crawling and I wanted to save that indignity till after he'd left.

Nicholas hung up and turned back to face me. His eyes were shocked and wide. 'Nicholas . . .?' What had been the final straw for him? Who had been on the phone?

'That was the hospital,' Nicholas said, reaching for my hand. He prised it from the wall and stepped in closer, trapping my palm between his chest and mine. 'I have to go.'

'Is it Olivia?'

He shook his head. 'Olivia's in surgery, I checked while you slept in the car. They're positive about her chances.' I groaned my relief. 'No . . . it's Norah.'

'They can't want you to identify her *now*. Can't it wait?'

Nicholas shook his head. 'You don't understand. They don't need me to identify her body. She's *awake*.'

'What?' This time my legs did go. Nicholas caught me with one arm. He still held my hand with the other.

'When the rift closed, I suppose enough of her life force returned – the energy the hounds had stolen – like yours did. She woke up in the ambulance. They managed to stabilise her.'

'Gran! Danny! Did you hear that?' I turned.

Danny skidded on the wooden floor, claws digging holes in the oak until he reached the hall rug which rucked under his feet. I noticed that in the light he was a kind of reddish-beige – it suited him. Gran leapt on to the sideboard.

'Norah's *alive*?' Gran miaowed.

Nicholas nodded. He pressed me back against the wall, his long thigh flat against mine. He let go of my hand and instead ran his fingers along my right shoulder and up the back of my neck. I shivered.

I could smell the remains of his expensive musky aftershave, almost overwhelmed by the sweat of the day's battle and the dark copper of the drying blood that had marked him. My eyes were level with the stubble that had become ragged over the course of the day. His veneer had gone.

I clung to him, unconsciously digging my own nails into his back. 'Go away Danny,' Nicholas growled.

Danny whined and slunk back towards the living room, followed swiftly by Gran.

'She'll need her job back.' Gran miaowed as her tail flicked around the corner. 'We've another mouth to feed now.'

Nicholas didn't look away from me; his dark eyes burned into mine. 'You're incredible, Ivy Mann,' he murmured, his lips so close to mine that I could taste his breath.

'You don't blame me?' I started.

Nicholas frowned. 'You made a mess and you cleaned it up. I respect that a lot. What happened to Norah . . .' He tailed off. 'Natalie would have got sick no matter what – *that* wasn't your fault. And if there hadn't been magic for her to mess with, after Natalie died, Norah would have self-destructed some other way. I wasn't paying attention and that's on me, *not* you.' He shook his head. 'Norah's alive because of you. A lot of kids are alive because you fought like the devil to save them.'

'You *don't* blame me.' I stared, and a weight I hadn't known I was carrying suddenly lightened. 'But . . .' I thought of the purple-haired girl. 'I didn't save everyone.'

'You did everything you could.' He started to stroke my neck.

'I'm not sexy,' I blurted in a rush.

'What?'

'I know what I look like.' I tried to gesture at my tracksuit bottoms, but my hand was trapped. 'You can't be interested in me, I'm not a model.'

'You think I care about that? Ivy, you *shine*.' Nicholas pressed his cheek on mine and inhaled slowly. His chest swelled against mine. He was in all my space. His fingers moved from my neck, into my hair. He dragged the band out of my ponytail and let it fall around my shoulders. His legs moved even closer, I no longer had to hold myself upright. I felt him smile.

Then he was pressing his lips to my check bone. Another kiss under my eye, another on the very edge of my lip. I shuddered. 'Ivy?' he asked.

I turned my head, just enough. I hardly had to move, he met me halfway. 'Yes.'

I guess there was some magic left in the world after all.

AFTERWARDS

NICHOLAS HAD LEFT and Gran and I were snuggled on the sofa with Danny at our feet. We were dozing and it was wonderful.

'Will you go back to the security job?' Gran asked.

'I'm not qualified for anything else,' I said. 'But with magic gone . . . will that job even exist? I don't—'

Danny whined suddenly, scrambled to his feet and raced for the bedroom. I frowned at Gran. When a frenzy of barking filled the air, I leapt up and hobbled stiffly after him.

Two men were climbing in through my bedroom window. I gaped.

Matilda was by my bed again, but one of them stood in front of the bedside table. When would I learn? I started to retreat.

'You know, my lock's broken. You could have come in the front door.'

The lead man shrugged. Too-small features were crowded into the centre of his face, as if his eyes and lips had tried to flee from his own hairline. But his mouth was wide and shark-like. 'Somebody wants very badly to speak to you. You've ruined some very important plans. Come quietly and we won't hurt your dog.' He aimed a kick at Danny who skidded out of the way with a furious snarl.

I was slow and unarmed. I staggered into the hallway and the men followed. 'Come on, now.'

Danny leapt at a thick pair of shoulders and was backhanded into the wall.

'Danny!' I screamed.

The lead man pulled out a gun.

I acted on instinct. '*Incensa!*' I raised a hand, feeling suddenly stupid. I was waving a gun loaded with blanks and everyone knew it.

But then I felt a familiar tugging.

'That won't work, thanks to you.' The man grinned

'*Incensa,*' I said again still walking backwards.

He laughed. 'Shouldn't have shut that rift, should you, girly?'

The skinnier one sniggered.

'*Incensa!*' Fire ripped from my fist and the men screamed. I screamed too, half horrified, half relieved. They fell backwards, beating at their clothes and hair. The skinny one fell to the ground rolling frantically, bouncing from wall to wall as he writhed.

'Get out!' Gran shrieked. Shark-teeth staggered towards the window, hit the glass and it shattered behind him. Burning, he crashed through and fell, screaming, to hit the railings below with a horrible final crunch.

I turned and threw my duvet over skinny, but he'd already stopped moving.

I stared at my hands. 'Gran . . . I didn't mean to. I didn't know. How did this happen? I thought we closed the rift.'

'You did. He said so.' Gran pushed me with her head and Danny caught hold of my trousers with his teeth. They dragged and pushed me until I backed into the sofa and collapsed. Danny licked my face with a whine.

'The rift closed,' Gran said, slowly. 'But you were right there in the middle of it.'

I stared at my hands in mute horror.

'I—vy,' Danny barked. 'No one. Can. Know.'

Gran crawled on to my lap. 'He's right. If anyone finds out what just happened . . .'

I put my head in my hands. 'How do we keep *this* a secret?'

Gran looked at the burn marks on the hall wall, at the body on my floor and then at my hands. Her mouth set in a grim line. 'Stand up, Ivy.'

I stood on shaking legs.

'Call the fire brigade, tell them there's been an explosion.' She looked around our flat one last time. 'Then start burning.'

ACKNOWLEDGEMENTS

SOMETIMES A BOOK is just so much fun to write that it flies off the ends of your fingertips, with characters who feel like best friends and lines that make you laugh or shiver.

This is that book for me.

The wonderful team at UCLAN, and especially my editor, Hazel Holmes, embraced Ivy and her story, and have made bringing her to all of you, another hugely enjoyable part of the process. (I wish they'd been around twenty-years ago, because I'd have loved to join their publishing course!)

As always, I'd like to say thank you to my agent, Catherine Pellegrino, who works tirelessly and believes in me unrelentingly.

And to my husband Andy, who encourages me to write, when I'm sure I could be earning real money doing something in an office. To my daughter Maisie, who makes me realise what a teenager can achieve when she puts her mind to something, and to my son Riley, who brings the good cheer and enthusiasm! You are all so inspiring.

This book has been birthed during a global pandemic. On my way to school drop-off I pass children in masks standing at the bus stop, I've barely seen my wider family in months (I miss them), and a trip to the supermarket is simultaneously fraught with nerves and an exciting day out! I would do almost anything to know that an end is in sight (right now, it's not) or that my children will not have their prospects annihilated by a recession the likes of which I've never seen in my lifetime (they likely will).

And I think of all those around me, feeling the same sense of disconnection, of loss, of confusion and grief.

Hopefully by the time *Raising Hell* hits the shelves, things will have changed for the better. There's little I can do to help, although I wish there was. What I can do is write a book for you that is enjoyable and keep writing, keep reaching out, keep connecting.

I hope you enjoyed it.

If so, do connect with me on Twitter: @BryonyPearce

And stay safe, stay well, keep shining.

IF YOU LIKED THIS,
YOU'LL LOVE . . .

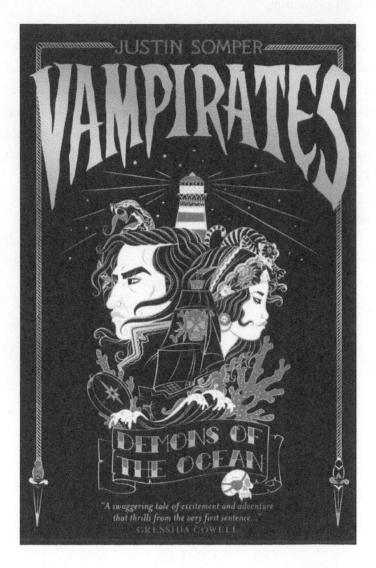

JUSTIN SOMPER

VAMPIRATES

DEMONS OF THE OCEAN

*"A swaggering tale of excitement and adventure
that thrills from the very first sentence..."*
CRESSIDA COWELL

ROSE EDWARDS

*This whole
kingdom floats
on a sea of blood*

*Plough the fields
and it comes
seeping up*

The
HARM TREE

"A rich, compelling epic" MELINDA SALISBURY

HAVE YOU EVER WONDERED HOW BOOKS ARE MADE?

UCLan Publishing are based in the North of England and involve BA Publishing and MA Publishing students from the University of Central Lancashire at every stage of the publishing process.

BA Publishing and MA Publishing students are based within our company and work on producing books as part of their course – some of which are selected to be published and printed by UCLan Publishing. Students also gain first-hand experience conceiving and running innovative high-level events to leverage sales, as well as running content creation business enterprises.

Our approach to business and teaching has been recognised academically and within the publishing industry. We have been awarded Best Newcomer at the Independent Publishing Guild Awards (2019) and a *Times* Higher Education Award for Excellence and Innovation in the Arts (2018).

As our business continues to grow, so too does the experience our students have upon entering UCLan Publishing.

To find out more, please visit
www.uclanpublishing.com/courses/